D1120951

For more information, address:
ZachEvans Creative LLC
601 N Ashley Drive Ste 1100-93513
Tampa, FL 33602
*info@zachevanscreative.com*

PRINTED IN THE USA.

*To Mo, who showed me Black Appalachia.*

# ACKNOWLEDGMENTS

Mom: It's almost ridiculous how much you support me. I can hardly wrap my mind around it. Making you proud is the best feeling. Thank you, I love you.

Angel: Remember when I figured out the ending for this while pacing back and forth in your room as you just sat there and let me talk incessantly at you? Yeah, thanks for that.

Ash: I know you like a man who can handle his liquor, so feel free to lust after Javier.

Stuff & Thangs Pals: I enjoy you horny nerds the most. Thank you for hyping me up and for believing in me. I can't wait until you're all here with me. Yes, even you, Nat.

Hawa: Thank you for supporting me, thank you for making me laugh, thank you for being my fave, and thank you for screaming with me about Michael Phan all the time.

Ify: Thank you for entertaining me with your shenanigans. You rock a jumpsuit and white hippie mom shoes better than anyone I know. Which, as you know, is a compliment.

Kat and Mina: I know I took forever to write this. Thank you for not hating me for it. Also, thank you for reading it first. For telling me what you liked, and where I was slacking. I owe you both a bunch of John Boyega-themed thirst tweets.

# MORE FROM JODIE SLAUGHTER

## All Things Burn: A BWWM Hitman Romance

*A woman forced to take dark, desperate measures for the sake of her safety seeks out a man who deals exclusively in doling out death sentences. What sparks between them is just as unavoidable as it is life-changing.*

Halle Temple is a good person; she doesn't know anything as surely as she knows that. A successful black woman who uses her expensive law degree to work full-time at a women's legal aid center, she has no doubt that her entire existence is being spent in the service of others. That perfectly normal life takes a deadly turn, however, when she crosses paths with a man who is willing to go to extreme measures to take possession of her.

After he sets his threats on her family, Halle begins to question every moral she has ever held dear as she realizes that there is only one way to get him out of her life for good. To do that, though, she needs a bit of help.

Callum Byrne is an Irish-American hitman who has made a life out of robbing others of their own. Darkness has always lurked inside of him and he has no qualms about setting it free - especially for profit. Halle enters his life suddenly, bringing with her an intensity that he has never felt before. It isn't long before Callum's narrow view of himself is twisted and challenged.

As the job she's given him becomes more complicated by the minute...so do Callum's feelings for her.

Order Now on Amazon

# WHITE WHISKEY BARGAIN

JODIE SLAUGHTER

ZEC PUBLISHING BY K. ALEX WALKER

# CHAPTER 1

HANNAH

Mama always said the real reason the moonshine business lasted so long after prohibition ended was because of how damned sexy it was. She wasn't wrong. People didn't care how grimy the process could be. They didn't care about the literal blood, sweat, and tears that went into that corn liquor they kept stashed away in their kitchen cabinets. There was no thought given to the runners who risked jail time by smuggling the product through the state and beyond. Those things may have been our dangerous reality, but to everyone else, they didn't even exist.

To the masses, moonshine was something shrouded in badly kept secrets, something just risky enough to be compelling. From the biggest cities in the state to counties still suffering under the collapse of coal country, people talked about moonshine—about *our* shine. Corn liquor so smooth and strong it made the Hawkins name synonymous with Harlan County, Kentucky.

For decades, that had been a great thing; it kept sales up

and morale high. In many ways, it still was. But it also made us a target.

Historically, our rivalries had been handled with as much civility as possible. Even still, the moonshine business wasn't clean in any form. It sometimes required dirty fighting, and while the Hawkins were good at being civil, we were even better at fighting dirty.

Reputation preceding, it had been going on two decades since we'd had anyone overstepping our battle lines. So, when I woke up weeks before to find one of my best and oldest runners bleeding out in his truck with the bed full of destroyed product, I knew our luck had finally run out. I wasn't banking on that luck magically returning to us, though, so I decided to drum up a plan that was a little more realistic.

Benicio Meza wasn't a very large man, but he had an incredibly imposing presence. His thick, hairy forearms rested on the dark wood tabletop as he attempted to stare me down. He had dark, sunken eyes and a crooked nose. A mouth that always seemed to be frowning. We were in the RedEye, a hole-in-the-wall bar halfway between Harlan and Cumberland, Kentucky. Clyde, my mother's right-hand man and I had made the short drive to the destination in good faith. Now, I wasn't so sure faith had been warranted.

Benicio had come alone, not bothering to bring any backup with him, which meant he didn't view me as a potential threat. In this particular scenario I wasn't, not to him, at least. But it made me feel like he didn't view me as a real adversary, like he didn't intend to take me seriously. In an attempt to mirror his slight, I'd requested Clyde stay out in the car for the duration of the meeting, bucking our normal tradition.

"I'm sorry we weren't able to make it to your mother's funeral," Benicio said. "We had a heavy shipment that required all hands on deck. I assume you got the flowers we sent?"

We were a little over a month separated from Mama's sudden and deadly stroke, and the open wound her passing left me with was still raw and hurting. As a leader, the fact that the Meza family hadn't paid their respects to her in the traditional way should have felt like a slight, and I assumed it was meant to be one. I didn't have the mental capacity to care much, though. The fact that Benicio's family hadn't been there to partake in my great aunt Mona's shitty potato salad meant next to nothing to me.

"Yes." I offered him a small smile. "I did. They were beautiful, thank you."

"Your mother was a good woman, a strong leader. Her presence would have been welcome in these difficult times."

Dick.

"That she was, but she did everything in her power to prepare me to follow in her footsteps. I might not ever live up to her name, but I'll have a hell of a time tryin'. That's why I wanted us to meet, so we can get ahead of this thing."

"Get ahead of it? Seems like it's already managed to get right in front of you."

He was referring to the shooting of Bobby Crenshaw, one of my family's best and most trusted shine runners. He'd been charged with smuggling a large shipment of product out of

3

Kentucky and into West Virginia. It was a trip he'd made count-less times, one that should have been quick and easy to complete. So when he didn't make the drop-off and suddenly stopped answering his phone, we knew something had gone wrong.

A small search team had been sent out to follow his trail. Luckily, they'd found him pretty quickly. If we had waited any longer to send people looking for him, he might have been dead.

Bobby had been shot twice in the stomach in the driver's seat of his truck on a less-traveled county road just outside of Harlan. The moonshine was still in crates in the back, completely untouched save for the presence of a horseshoe off to the side. When the men brought it back to me, it was clear that it was new—the shiny silver gleamed and the name *Ward* was clearly inscribed on the front in bold letters.

Bobby had been taken to an emergency room close by and when the police had come asking questions, he'd told them he'd been mugged and hadn't seen the guys who did it. It was a lie, obviously, as he'd described the man who shot him to me perfectly—a tall white man with greasy brown hair, a tattoo of a bird on his neck, and a silver front tooth. I'd put people on trying to find the man, but the man was a ghost. We at least knew who he worked for, which meant we knew who was coming after us. Who we needed to go after.

"Yeah, we had an incident. One that left a member of my organization nearly dead, but I wouldn't say these guys have gotten the upper hand yet."

Benicio didn't scoff, but he screwed his face up a bit, the

dimple in his chin deepening. "I disagree. Somethin' like this could have been easily avoided had your family heeded the warnin' signs."

"Warnin' signs?" I tried hard not to let the insult color my tone. I didn't succeed. "What warnin' signs? You mean the rumors around town that some new family was about to be comin' for our heads?"

"The very one."

I waved a hand in front of my face. "Rumors about the *big white boogeyman* comin' to take our spot have been floatin' around these parts since my great granddaddy cooked up his first batch of shine, Mr. Meza. I'm sure you can relate since your family hears the same ones."

"That's true, Miss Hawkins." He chuckled. "But these were different."

"How so?" I was becoming increasingly annoyed with the direction of the conversation. I wanted to get back to the meat of it, but I didn't have the same finesse my mama did when it came to manipulating conversations in her favor. Not yet anyway.

So, I let him talk.

"It was clear these weren't just rumors the second the Ward family name started comin' up. Maybe you're too young to know exactly what's behind that name, or maybe your mama ain't have time to teach it to you but—"

"Oh, I know who the Wards are, Mr. Meza. You forget, I went to school in Lexington where that name rings plenty of bells. I just assumed they'd use all that old coal money they have to stick to racin' horses or whatever else they get into. Not try to terrorize all us poor folk."

"Come on now," he chided, almost playfully. "You know there ain't anythin' rich people like more than terrorizin' poor folk."

He was right. It was a statement history had proven true time and time again.

"You got me there," I conceded. "But that doesn't mean those rumors were credible. I mean, apparently, they weren't credible enough for you to tighten up your ranks. A few of your runners just got their product jacked by some guys from the Ward family, right?"

He looked down at the table for a few moments before he looked back up at me with his jaw steeled and eyes hard. "Maybe, but they all came out unharmed, unlike Bobby Crenshaw."

"Probably because they view your family as less of a threat," I bit out.

"Well, your mama sure seemed to view us as a threat."

I shrugged, picking at my unpainted fingernails. "I think it's more likely she just viewed you as a nuisance."

Benicio's lips moved into a sneer, and I cursed myself. Rival or not, the man was my elder and I held a level of respect for him. It went against everything I'd ever been taught to speak to him the way I was. But damn if I was going to sit there and let him talk shit about my family. Either way, we weren't there to exchange thinly veiled insults and petty jabs. We were there to come up with a solution for our mutual issue.

My mother's image flashed in my mind in an instant, her dark brown face turned downward in reproach. It was the same look she'd given me my entire life anytime I got too quick on the draw with my words.

I took a deep breath, clamping the teeth on the right side of my mouth down together almost painfully as I retreated. Swallowing and looking up at him with softened eyes, I forced myself into humbleness. Now, I couldn't help but resent the responsibilities my mother had left me unprepared to handle.

"Excuse me." I cleared my throat. "I apologize. This ain't what we're here for."

He stared me down silently for a few moments before flashing me a small smile. It wasn't genuine, but it showed me he was struggling with reining in his pride too.

"You're right. Old rivalries are hard to work through, but we've got to if we want to make it out of this shit alive."

"Exactly." I clasped my hands on the table, mirroring him and leaned forward a bit. "Whether warnin' signs were heeded or not, it's too late now, for both of us, and we need to do something about it."

"What are you suggestin'?"

"Mr. Meza, I believe there's only one way to keep the Wards from destroying the businesses both of our families have worked hard to build. If we don't work together, they're goin' to pick us apart. They have the money, the power, the influence, and obviously, the willingness to hurt our people. I want to avoid either of us having to bury anybody." It was the strongest, surest thing I'd said throughout the meeting, and Benicio's impressed expression proved it.

"You think we should join forces?"

"Yes." I nodded. "It's unconventional, I know, but I've been thinkin' on it and it's the only system that seems like it could actually work. We can keep our actual productions separate but come together in other ways. I'll send some of my people over to Cumberland and you can send some to Harlan. They'll double up for more manpower on runs and we can increase security in our production houses. Hell, we can even get some guys to camp out at bars to keep those bastards from trying to intimidate local clients."

"There is strength in numbers," he said quietly.

"Exactly," I replied. "They may have plenty of advantages over us, but we have the numbers to put up one hell of a fight. Only together though."

"And what are you thinkin' in terms of the cost when it comes to this new partnership?"

I leaned back in my chair and smiled. I knew I had him. "That's the best part, Mr. Meza. It would cost next to nothin'. We can treat it like a temp agency—I hire my guys out to you and I pay them like I always would out of my own pockets and vice versa. We can split any additional costs down the middle."

"We'll need to stock up on weapons." He crossed his arms over his chest. "That'll be an added cost."

I didn't like it, but I knew it would be necessary. Up until the presence of the Wards, the moonshine business around our parts had been almost completely violence-free for decades.

Especially while wading through the murky waters of federal laws making moonshine legal and state laws bucking back against that ruling. The rivalry between our families may have been strong, but Mama and Mr. Meza had ensured we could live in relative peace anyway. I knew that peace was finally coming to an end. Only, it wouldn't be the Mezas we'd be fighting.

"That's fine. Sheriff Neal's share of our profits will need to be upped if we want him to continue turning the other way with the increased presence in Harlan."

Benicio nodded. "He'll want the same from us."

"I'll have Clyde prepare an official expense sheet, but as I said, you shouldn't have to come out of your pockets too much."

Once again, he nodded. Assuming our meeting was over, I stood from my seat and reached a hand out, preparing to shake to make our tenuous partnership official. Only, Benicio didn't return the gesture.

"What's wrong?" I asked.

"Your plan is good, Miss Hawkins, and it could work. But there's a lot of history between our families. How am I supposed to trust you won't betray us if you get the chance?"

I shrugged. "The same way I'll have to trust you won't screw me over. We both have to have faith."

Benicio laughed loud and hard from his belly. I bit the inside of my cheek to keep from sneering or saying something brash and foolish.

"Please, Hannah." It was the first time he used my first

name. "I know you're new to this, but you can't be that naive."

"Faith is naive now?" I asked. Mama may have been a staunch realist, but even she had understood the value of having a certain amount of faith.

"When you've got lives on the line as we do, yeah, faith is naive," he answered. "If we're goin' to join our families up, there's only one way we can eliminate the possibility of betrayal. And that's through the old way."

Vague as the phrasing was, I understood what he meant immediately. It was something that had been done to tie families together for centuries. Whether it was for money, protection, or status, marriage was probably the oldest binding agent in the world. It wasn't something done around our parts much anymore, but it definitely wasn't an eliminated practice.

Transactional marriages.

My heart sputtered. I looked silently over at Benicio. I'd spent days preparing for our meeting, all but rehearsing my spiel word-for-word and even practicing the schooling of my features in my bathroom mirror. I was prepared for pushback. Hell, I was even prepared for rejection, but I hadn't been at all prepared for a proposal.

"You," I cleared my throat when my voice came out weak, "you're married."

Benicio's eyes widened, his dark, busy brows jumping up high on his forehead. "Not to me, good God. To Javier, my son."

Javier. Jesus. I knew of him, of course, I did. Neither Harland or Cumberland, where the Meza family was stationed, was very big, nor were they very far apart. It didn't matter how intensely our families had tried to remain separate, I'd run into Javier Meza a few times. I'd never had more than a brief conversation with him, but I remembered him well enough, tall and rugged with tawny brown skin and a presence that made him impossible to ignore.

"I thought Javier was married too," I offered lamely.

Last I'd heard, Javier had married a woman from Lexington who was close to his mother's side of the family. I knew as much about her as I did about him, which was next to nothing.

Benicio waved a dismissive hand in front of his face. "They split up a couple of years ago."

I sighed, crossing my arms across my chest, looking over at him silently. I hadn't spent a ton of time thinking about marriage, but whenever I had, I always assumed I'd just kind of fall ass-backward into it. Like many people, I figured it was one of those facets of life that was unavoidable, like death. Whenever I thought about the man I'd be inevitably be tying myself to, it was always just some nameless, faceless shape of a person. A marriage of convenience had never crossed even crossed my mind as a possibility. Still, there I was, actively considering the prospect of one.

It wasn't something I necessarily wanted to do, but I didn't think my wants mattered anymore. When Mama died, she'd been sure to leave me in charge of the family business. I was a leader now, and being a leader meant making hard decisions, especially when you were the one who had to bear the brunt of them.

If my people wanted to survive the threat looming over us, we needed to join forces with the Mezas. With so much bad blood between our families, there was no way we could work together if we didn't establish trust. As fucked up as it may have been, Benicio was right—we needed to be bound to one another, literally. Besides, it may have been a tradition left-over from the old world in our community, but we lived in the twenty-first century. Once we got the Wards out of the picture, it would only be a few strokes of a pen to make a divorce happen. Hopefully, as soon as possible.

"And Javier would be willin' to do this?" I asked.

"Javier knows what his responsibilities are," he said slowly. "I will speak with my son about it today, but I have no doubt he'll understand the importance of this union."

"Fine. You get back to me with his answer tonight, and then we'll meet to negotiate our terms."

"What kind of terms?"

"I don't know. I haven't thought of them yet."

# CHAPTER 2

JAVIER

The last time I'd seen Hannah Hawkins she'd been pumping gas at a service station in Winchester, Kentucky. It had only been a couple of months since my divorce and I'd been heading to Lexington for the first time since to see my grandmother. I had no idea where Hannah was heading, but I'd recognized her immediately. My view of her had only lasted a few seconds as she made long, confident strides from the store to her car. If she saw me, she didn't acknowledge it, and I'd had no reason to approach her either. The non-exchange was something I'd almost forgotten about completely until I sat across the table from her in her house in Harlan.

Hannah was, undoubtedly, an incredibly beautiful woman. Her skin was a few shades darker than mine, a captivating brown that reminded me of a deeply shaded amber stone my mother had when I was a kid. Her dark eyes were inviting, almost sweet, and posed the perfect juxtaposition to the stern look on her face. I was torn between feeling intrigued and scrutinized all at once.

Mami and Pop sat on either side of me, and next to her sat her younger sister and a man I didn't know. The room was quiet except for the large metal fan whirring away in the corner of the dining room. I tried my damndest not to stare Hannah down like a creep, but I couldn't seem to keep my eyes off her for more than a few seconds at a time. Not even just because she was gorgeous, either, but because I could barely wrap my head around the fact that I was going to be marrying her.

The tension of our awkward silence was finally cut when my mother cleared her throat. "Right," she said, just loud enough for the entire table to hear her. "We might as well go on ahead and get this thing started, no sense in sitting here like ducks."

Across from me, Hannah nodded, her wavy, chin-length hair shifting with her movements. "You're absolutely right, Mrs. Meza. The sooner we get this done, the sooner we can get the ball rollin' on our other plans."

She reached down to pick up the glass of water in front of her, those brown fingers shaking a bit as they wrapped around the sweating cup. We all waited silently as she took a sip, then another, before speaking again.

"So..." She looked directly at me. "Javier, I take it since you're here now, you've agreed to this arrangement?"

"Yes, I've agreed to marry you, Miss Hawkins."

"So easily? It's barely been a day since your daddy and I discussed it."

"I imagine I have the same reasons you do, ma'am. My

family is in danger too and if this is the only way to protect us all then so be it."

Hannah kept her eyes on mine, the warm, syrupy coloring making it impossible for me to look away. After a few moments, she broke her gaze with a tight smile. "Well, I guess if we're goin' to be married, you can stop callin' me *ma'am*."

"All right, just Hannah, then."

She swallowed and looked at both my parents. "Aside from me and Javier, I know everybody else is mostly here because of tradition and formality and all that other shit. So, before he and I get our time alone to work out our terms, is there anything y'all want to request?"

"Children," my father said immediately.

Hannah's eyes widened, and her shoulders shifted a little bit straighter against the back of her chair. "What about them?"

"Well," Pop spared a glance at me, "I assume you won't be takin' the Meza name."

"Absolutely not," she answered with force.

Pop's jaw tightened. "Which is why I'd like to request that any children that come from this union be given the Meza name."

"And why would I agree to that?"

"The only reason we're here is because you understand how important our family legacies are, Miss Hawkins. Javier is my only child, the only way our name can be carried on."

"So the Hawkins name means nothing then?" It was her sister who interjected this time.

Pop raised his hands in a defensive manner. "Of course

that's not what I'm sayin,' but you have your sister here and any kids she may have can carry on the Hawkins name. I only had sisters. Sisters who took the names of their husbands."

Hannah's top lip curled, and I watched as the man next to her reached out to lay a hand on her shoulder. I got the feeling he was protecting us from her more than he was trying to prevent her from offending us.

"Of course, I feel sorry for your situation, Mr. Meza, but I'm offended you would ask me to give children that I carry and birth your name for reasons that don't concern me."

"Oh, you'll be a part of our family real soon, Miss Hawkins, so I'd say it should concern you too."

She laughed. "I seriously doubt—"

"All right, y'all, all right!" I sat up straighter. "It's twenty-nineteen. We can solve this shit very easily. Any uh…" I coughed. "Any kids that Hannah and I have can just take both our names. Mexican people have been doing that for hundreds of years, Pop. It's not like it's somethin' uncommon."

Hannah's eyes narrowed at me for a split second before she looked back at my father. "I can make that work if you can."

Pop sniffed, the same sharp, short sound he made whenever he was trying to keep himself from saying what he really wanted to.

"Fine."

That tight smile was back on Hannah's face as she sat back, only this time, it was given with an added amount of smugness. "Great. Now that that's settled, I think it's time for Javier and me to discuss the rest of our terms by ourselves."

Long, hesitant glances were shared between our two groups before Hannah and I were finally left alone. She didn't let the silence between us last for more than a moment before she spoke to me directly.

"So, I guess I'll just go first then?"

"Sure." I pulled a piece of paper out of the back pocket of my jeans and carefully unfolded it. When I didn't hear her continue, I looked up to see her staring at me, her lips parted in shock. "What?"

"You brought a list? An actual handwritten list?"

I frowned. "This is important. I didn't want to forget my terms."

"Important?" Her eyebrows raised. "Javier, I'm not tryin' to be an asshole here, but you realize this marriage is a formality, right? We just need to do this so we can squash some of the bad blood between our families. This ain't no love match, honey."

"Oh, trust me, I know."

"Do you?"

"Hannah, I'm not an idiot. I don't love you any more than you love me. But that doesn't mean we can't go into this thing with some kind of respect for each other. Besides, I might be a two-time divorcee soon. Can you cut me some damn slack?"

She smiled. This time, it was genuine and filled with humor. "Fine," she drawled. "You go on ahead first then, with your little list."

I couldn't help but chuckle.

"I really just have a few," I started. "First, I want us to have an actual celebration after the wedding. The Mezas love to party and it would be a good time for our people to officially come together for the first time without too much static."

Hannah nodded, her eyes towards the ceiling as she considered my request. "Okay, we can do that. That's a good idea actually."

I smiled. "Second, I get that this marriage ain't like other ones and never will be and that's fine, but I want us to live together and I want us to have dinner together at least three times a week."

Those delicately arched eyebrows of hers raised up nearly into her hairline again. "Three times a week?"

"You don't have dinner with your family?"

I found it hard to believe she didn't. Obviously, I didn't know much about the Hawkins family, but everyone knew how close they were. Like everyone in our communities, tradition and family history were more important than most things. Even the situation Hannah and I had found ourselves in was something left over from old-world customs. If I'd been asked to, I would have put money down on the knowledge that Hannah Hawkins ate dinner with her family almost every night growing up, especially Sundays.

"We used to." She put a fist to her mouth and cleared her throat. "But I haven't been around much the last couple years and then Mama died so…"

"Oh, right."

I felt like an asshole immediately.

"But," she continued, "I guess I can make that happen three nights a week. You cook right?" She looked at me sharply. "Because there ain't no way I'm cookin' every time just because you're lazy or you have some fucked up view of—"

"Yes, I cook. Really well, actually. My granddaddy owned a restaurant in Lexington when I was growin' up and I used to cook with him."

A sly smirk slid over Hannah's lips. "So, I get my own personal chef then?"

"No." I stared her down. "You get a husband who is happy to make you a hot meal anytime you want one."

"I guess I can get on board with that too."

She ran a tongue over her lips and her neck contracted as she swallowed. My eyes narrowed just a bit as I watched her lids become a little heavier. Her reaction was subtle, but I couldn't be sure. In any other scenario, I would have sworn she was showing desire, but I'd never even caught a whiff of that from Hannah in my direction.

Instead of working myself up thinking on it, I chalked it all up to tiredness and moved on. "Right. Last thing and I'm done." I took a glance at my list again. "I want us to *try*."

"Try what?"

"This, us. Like I said before, I know we ain't in love and I don't expect us to ever fall in love, but I want us to be good to each other. People have been gettin' married in situations like this for hundreds of years and they've made it work. It doesn't matter if this doesn't last forever. I'm goin' to make sure I'm good to you, and I'd appreciate it if you extended me the same courtesy."

With my heart in my throat, I folded the piece of notebook

paper back up and stuffed it deep into the pocket I'd pulled it from.

"I..." She stopped abruptly and closed her eyes tight. "I don't know how to be a good wife, Javier."

"And I don't know how to be a good husband, but we can try."

Her eyebrows furrowed. "You've been married though."

My molars ground together, and my nails dug into the palms of my hands as my past failure was brought to the forefront of our conversation. "I know, and I wasn't a good husband, which is why I'm here now, divorced."

Hannah's eyes widened at my admission. For a second, I thought she'd try to get me to speak on it more. Dread washed over me but, once again, she rolled over my expectations and let the subject drop completely.

"That's all I ask." I gave her a smile I hoped was comforting.

"I guess it's my turn then?" Hannah smiled back. "I don't have many either. Number one," she extended her pointer finger, "we don't meddle in each other's business more than necessary. I think that'll make things easier, you know. After."

It was a logical request, one I had no issue complying with. "That's fine with me."

"Good to know." Her middle finger went out. "Number two, no sleepin' with other people while we're together. I don't need you out here embarrassin' me when people think we're an actual couple so keep your parts in your drawers."

A deep laugh escaped me before I could stop it. "Are you serious?"

"Yes. Don't think you can abstain for a few months?"

"Oh, I've got no problem with that. Never had a problem keepin' my dick to myself when needed. I just didn't think you'd agree to some shit like this." I crossed my arms over my chest.

"Oh, I'm not," she deadpanned.

My teeth clamped together again. I liked Hannah, honestly. She was bold and straightforward, and I appreciated that she didn't mince words much, but it also seemed like she tended to push too far in an effort to steamroll people. I may have been a levelheaded guy normally, but I wouldn't be walked all over.

"Let me get this straight. You, rightfully, don't want me to makin' a mess of this by throwing' dick around town, but I'm supposed to be cool with you doin' the same shit to me?"

Hannah leaned forward so our faces were closer together. She stared into my eyes, and I could see by the hard set in her jaw she was also growing more irritated. "Only, I wouldn't be embarrassing you," she said. "I know how to be discreet." Her tone was dripping in condescension.

"Nah." I shook my head. "I don't care how discreet you think you can be. We don't set rules for each other that we won't follow ourselves. This shit is equal, Hannah Hawkins. If I don't get to fuck until we're through, you don't either."

Those big eyes of hers widened, presumably in response to the finality in my tone. It nearly made me want to fold, but I refused to, on principal. I was less concerned about Hannah "embarrassing" me by sleeping with someone else and more concerned with the major imbalance she was trying to create in our new relationship.

"Fuck."

"I'm sorry, Hannah, but fair is fair. If you want to get rid of that term altogether, we can." My shoulders suddenly tensed.

Her eyes flew to mine, a gaze nearly hot enough to set me on fire. "I can handle it," she said. "Fine, fine. I'll just...put my libido on pause for a little while."

I raised an eyebrow but said nothing.

"Let's just move on. It's probably my most important one, and we're already halfway there since you said you wanted us to live together." She stopped to take another sip of her water, and I could see small beads of sweat forming on her forehead. "I'm fine with livin' with you, Javier, but I want it to be in my house." She gestured around us. "In this house."

The Hawkins house was famous in our part of the woods. Word was that Hannah's great granddaddy had built it for her great grandmother with shine money. People said it took him months to make everything perfect for the woman. Then, when it was finished, he had men stand guard around it day and night to keep all the angry racists in the area from trying to burn it down. Obviously, it worked. The house was old, but decades later it was clear it had been a source of pride in the Hawkins family. Big and white, the damn thing was just as gorgeous as it was imposing.

I liked the house I lived in just fine, but it was full of memories, some good and others downright awful. I'd bought it cheap when I was young and fixed it up as best as I could.

My ex-wife, Mari, moved in with me after we got married, and when she left me four years later, I stayed. It wasn't a sentimental connection that tied me to the place but complacency instead. I was positive it would be strange laying my head somewhere other than where I had almost every night for almost ten years, but I was willing to give it a try.

"That sounds fine to me," I said with a small smile. "That it or you got any more?"

"Uh…" She coughed. "That's it."

"You sure?"

"If I come up with anything else before the wedding, I'll let you know."

"And when is our wedding goin' to be?"

"I'll call the courthouse and make an appointment for two weeks from today." She chuckled. "County clerk's website says we can sign our marriage license that day. You think that's enough time for you to plan your little after-party?"

I laughed with her, suddenly feeling just a little lighter and much more anxious at the same time. "You're going to get enough of callin' me little, Hannah Hawkins."

"Oh, I doubt it, Javier." Her full cheeks puffed up a bit when she grinned. "That goofy face you make when I do it brings me way too much fuckin' joy to ever stop."

# CHAPTER 3

HANNAH

"What do you think Mama would say about this dress if she was here right now?" I asked my younger sister as we stood in front of a floor-length mirror in my bedroom.

Nicole snorted. "She'd say you were showin' too much leg and not enough breast."

The laugh I released was choked and wet. Nicole was exactly right. A few days after our marriage negotiations, I'd been in Louisville looking at some new parts for our distilling machines with Clyde. While I was there, I'd gone to one of their fancier bridal thrift stores looking for a wedding dress. I'd had a hard time finding something that fit me, literally and figuratively, flipping through racks of pristine white gowns covered in lace and frills. It wasn't until I gave up and was ready to leave the store altogether and buy something online that I actually found a dress worth trying on.

It was white but a slightly off-cream color. It came to right above my knees and the bodice and skirt were very tame, fitting up top with gentle waves. But it was the neckline, chest, and arms that made me fall in love with it. It had a gentle sweet-heart line that essentially hid my considerable cleavage. The chest and arms were covered in a gauzy white lace that rested at my elbows. It was relatively simple, but still so beautiful I felt selfish for choosing to wear it on my sham of a wedding day.

However, I'd realized as I'd stared at my reflection, I couldn't bring myself to regret my choice too much. I'd deserved at least one beautiful thing for making such a big sacrifice.

"Yeah, you're right," I choked out, turning around to face my sister. "She probably would've hated it."

Nicole shook her head, tears welling up in the corner of her eyes. "No, she would've bitched about it, but she would've told you that you look beautiful. You do, sis. You look so beautiful today."

All I could do was give her a small smile. My head fully understood this marriage wasn't sentimental, but my heart still hurt whenever I thought about the fact my mother wouldn't be there to see me enter into it.

Both of us were startled out of our thoughts by a quiet knock on the opened door. Clyde stood on the other side, his tall, slim frame outfitted in a pair of simple slacks and a button-down shirt.

"We need to go if we're goin' to get there on time." He smiled at me. "You don't want to set this thing off with a late start."

His features went from smiling to sullen by the time he got all his words out. I frowned too, knowing exactly what he was thinking. Clyde had never outwardly expressed his displeasure at the situation I'd found myself in, but I'd known him long enough to decipher his little looks.

Clyde Miller had grown up side-by-side with my mother. Orphaned after his parents died in a car accident, my grandmama, Thea, had taken him in. Everyone who worked with and for the Hawkins family was considered family, but Clyde was literally family. The man was a pillar of strength and support, and he'd essentially acted as mine and Nicole's father after ours had run down the mountain for good.

Clyde thought I was making a mistake. Before I'd decided to propose joining with the Mezas, Clyde and I had spent hours trying to come up with a solution to the threat we were facing. He'd thrown out many plans, even one that began and ended with trying to pay off the people who were trying to take us down. Just the thought of it made me mad enough to spit.

*"We don't need any more blood spilled over this,"* Clyde said, teeth gritted. *"Your mama's already gone. You so eager to follow her into an early grave?"*

*"Well, if you're lookin' to get us to roll over and show our bellies to a bunch of our enemies, we might as well do it to someone who can help us beat these bastards."*

He'd been unhappy when I'd requested a meeting with Benicio Meza, frustrated when that meeting had taken place, and furious when I'd left the meeting having arranged a marriage for myself. In the weeks since, Clyde must have tried to get me to take back my agreement to marry Javier a hundred times. It never worked, though, and I could see him gearing up for one last attempt.

"Hannah," he breathed. "Please, let's—

"Do this." My voice was as strong as I could muster right now. "You're right, Clyde. I don't want to be late."

The ride to the Harlan County Clerk's Office was a short, quiet one. By the time Nicole, Clyde, my best friend, Lex, and I reached the front entrance, Javier was already standing out front with a small group of family members. Our so-called reception was set for that evening. In typical style, we were having a barn party. With music, food, and more moonshine than any person should safely drink, the Meza and Hawkins families were set to get together for the first time. I hoped we could keep things peaceful, but I wasn't hedging any bets on it. If we made it through the night with less than three fights, I'd consider it a success.

For the actual ceremony, we kept it tight. I only invited three people. Javier invited a couple of cousins and his best friend, Adrian, along with his parents. That was it. Eight people would watch me get married—an incredibly small number—and I was still sweating bullets.

"Wait, hold up," Lex called from beside me as we made our way from the side parking lot.

"What's wrong?"

"Are you tryin' to sweat your way through that dress?"

"Shit," I groaned. "You can tell?"

She pulled a hand mirror out of her purse and handed it to me. I could see the wetness beading up on my forehead and temples. It was early May and barely seventy-five degrees outside. On top of that, my dress was the furthest thing from heavy. I knew my anxiousness was the cause. I also knew there was no way I could stop it.

"If you're not trying to sweat your hair out, you need to stop and let me get you together before you go in there." Lex started rooting around in her bag again.

"Here." Clyde handed her a pristine white handkerchief. She gave him a quick, "Thanks" and immediately started dabbing my forehead with it.

"Damn, my makeup," I whined. I'd spent nearly an hour watching one of those online tutorials in an attempt to get my eye to look just right. I hated that it was probably going to be ruined because of my overactive sweat glands.

"It's fine," Lex insisted. "You can't even notice any of it came off. Just calm down, take some deep breaths or somethin'."

I shut up and did as she said, sucking the clean air deep into my lungs and releasing it. The action didn't make me feel any better, but it did calm my speeding heart some.

"I'm ready," I said after a few moments of silence. "The quicker this gets done, the quicker I can get to drinkin'."

Javier and his family were huddled in a small circle when we reached them. His dark eyes widened when he finally looked up at me.

"Hannah." He broke rank to come stand in front of me. "Good mornin'."

"Mornin'," I answered.

He continued to stare.

"You look beautiful, Hannah," Alma Meza said to me with a warm smile. "Truly."

Mrs. Meza's voice was incredibly comforting. It had the smooth, warm lilt of a mother who loved. Her accent was distinctly Kentuckian but significantly less pronounced than those of us who had grown up in the mountains. She'd grown up in Lexington but moved to Cumberland to be with Mr. Meza. She'd been in Appalachia for more than thirty years and had barely managed to pick up any of the spoken eccentricities. It was different, but it was still calming, so I let it wash over me.

"Thank you, ma'am." I stood with my hands tightly clutching my purse in front of me. "So, do you. I love the flower in your hair."

She was perfect, dressed in her Sunday best. I briefly wondered how it felt for her to dress up so prettily for her son's doomed marriage. And his second one at that.

"You look very handsome as well, Benicio." I glanced up at Javier. "And you, Javier."

Benicio gave me a small smile. Javier's was bigger, all teeth and crinkled eyes.

My tongue immediately felt heavy in my mouth. I swallowed harshly. He'd kept his beard short from where it connected to the sides of his head and thicker around his jaws and upper lip. His light brown skin was smooth and clear, and he wore a black suit on his tall, lean body.

*Fuck.*

My future husband cut a very fine figure, and I hated it

just as much as I loved it. I forced myself to look away for a second.

"You're unbelievable, Hannah. Beautiful enough to make a man forget his words."

Even with the morning sun beating down on me, a shiver ran through my body. His voice wasn't incredibly deep, but it was rough, and the way his words slanted as he said them almost made me forget mine did the same.

"You didn't, though," I joked.

"You see it took me a while to get my mouth workin' to speak, don't you?"

"I was just chalkin' that up to your quiet nature."

We were nervous, and the situation was tense, but Javier and I shared a small smile that made the atmosphere a little lighter.

After our group made a round of general introductions, we made our way inside. While our families waited in the lobby, he and I stood in front of the clerk's desk, shoulder to shoulder with our most important documents in hand. We tried our hardest to present the picture of a happy, loving couple as the clerk processed our information.

Javier, ever the gentleman, offered to pay the thirty-five-dollar processing fee, but as she slid the certificate across the counter towards us to sign, I hoped I didn't look nearly as terrified as I felt.

"Here it is," she said with a wide smile. "The best part. All I need is your signatures, and then we can have the officiant meet you for the ceremony."

"You first," I choked out, all but shoving the document in Javier's direction.

His large hands gripped the shitty black pen we'd been provided, his knuckles pale from the pressure. My forehead started sweating again the second the pen touched the paper. It took seconds for Javier to scrawl out his name, and the bold, choppy cursive suddenly became the most terrifying thing I'd ever seen.

His warm fingers brushed mine as he handed me then pen, and I gulped down some air in an attempt to calm my nerves. I needed to remind myself why the hell I was doing this, why I was legally binding myself to a man I didn't love. A man I knew next to nothing about.

*Family.*

*Security.*

*Legacy.*

The words meant everything to me. They were at the backbone of my entire life. The Hawkins had managed to make a way when there had been no way. In a place they weren't wanted, and in a time they weren't even seen as human beings, they'd managed to create something strong and lasting and beautiful. I refused to let it be taken away from us, to have that history tainted and forgotten.

I thought about the sacrifices my own mother had made, ones different from the one I was about to commit myself to but still hard as hell. Joy Hawkins would have married someone she didn't love in a second if she knew it offered her the chance to save the family. She would have signed the damned papers and be done with it without even bothering to look back and regret it later. I needed to get my shit together. I needed to be like her.

My teeth clacked together in a painful clench. I quickly scrawled my signature out on the designated line. The letters were thin, neat, and loopy, a pale imitation of my grandmother's perfect cursive.

I couldn't bring myself to look over at Javier as I handed the paper back over to the clerk. Even when she got up to file it away and make copies, I kept my eyes on the off-white wall straight ahead.

It was his touch that finally made me put eyes on him, large and warm and slightly calloused. He placed his hand on top of mine where it rested on the counter. He didn't intertwine our fingers, instead tucking his underneath the wide space between my index and thumb.

"We did the right thing," he said softly.

I didn't know whether he was trying to convince me or himself. Either way, I didn't think he was successful.

"Maybe it'll start feelin' like it soon."

"It will."

This time, his soft voice had so much conviction, I couldn't help but flash him a small smile.

"All right," the smiling woman said as she returned to her seat. I pulled my hand away from Javier's and hung my arms at my side.

"Here are copies of the license." Her eyes strayed behind us. "And there's the officiant."

Javier and I turned to see a tall bald man with brown skin and a short white beard.

"Hannah Hawkins and Javier Meza?" he asked with his eyes slightly widened. If he recognized us or our names, he didn't speak on it. I appreciated that. "Y'all ready?"

"Let me just..." I walked, briskly, to the door and stuck my head out into the lobby where our families were silently waiting. I waved them in then ran back to Javier's side.

"Right," the man drawled. "My name is Don Bailey. Just to let you know, I ain't a preacher or a judge, just a county clerk. So, if you want one of them to marry y'all today, you're goin' to have to provide your own and come back within thirty days."

"Uh..." I coughed. "No, you'll do just fine, Mr. Bailey."

"Good, let's get this thing rollin' so we can have you folks out of here, yeah?" He smiled.

It was a joke, a funny one judging by the laughs of our families, but neither Javier nor I joined in.

Don pulled out a bible.

"I'm supposed to touch that?" I asked.

"That's normally how it goes, ma'am."

"Well, all right." I swallowed. "But if I burst into flames, I'm goin' to haunt my new husband until he sues you, Mr. Bailey."

I heard my sister snort from her place next to me. Even Don let out a little chuckle. Javier put his hand down first and it was large enough that it covered the majority of the Bible. With my hand on top of his, only my thumb touched the worn leather.

"You two got any vows you want to say?"

I looked over at Javier and he looked back at me. His eyes

were dark brown, and I had to stop myself from sinking into the feeling they gave me.

He subtly shook his head at me, and I turned back to Don. "No, sir."

"Well, I need y'all to repeat after me then." Don looked straight at me. "I do solemnly declare that I know no lawful reason why I, Hannah Hawkins, may not be joined in matrimony with Javier Meza."

I repeated the words stronger than I thought I would and then waited for Javier's turn.

"We got plenty of witnesses here today. Good. That means I don't have to go draggin' somebody in here." Don looked around at the small cluster of the family we'd brought. "Hannah, repeat after me again, please. 'I call upon these persons here present to witness that I, Hannah Joy Hawkins, do take thee, Javier Alexander Nicolas Meza, to be my lawfully wedded husband.'"

Seconds after he recited them, I regurgitated them back. Keeping my eyes on Javier's, I used the strength and surety in his gaze to bolster my own.

"By the power of the state of Kentucky, I pronounce you lawfully wedded," Don said, the air of authority in his voice making the pronouncement even more startling.

It was an incredibly short ceremony. After he made his declaration, Don tucked the Bible into his side and shot us a small smile. "If that'll be all, I have some paperwork to get back to."

"Yes sir," Javier answered. "That's all we need. I thank

you for takin' the time out of your day to join me and my wife together."

Fuck.

*My wife.*

That designation was going to take a while to get used to. Honestly, I wasn't sure if I would ever comfortably settle into it. Javier didn't seem to have nearly as much trouble with it as I did, and I didn't know how to feel about that either.

Nicole had to virtually hold my body up with her arm wrapped around mine as we left the courthouse. Our small group was awkwardly quiet as we stood around in a circle outside.

"You two did good in there." Surprisingly, it was Clyde who broke the silence. "Hannah, your mama would have been proud."

Clyde knew my mother better than anyone in the world, even me. Every single one of my recent actions had been made with the purpose of doing right by all the hard work my mother had put into our family. Having the person who had been closest to her while she did that work recognize me in that way had me grinning despite my jumbled feelings.

"Thank you, Clyde." I reached out to hug him. He'd been wearing the same cologne since I could remember, and the scent of it on his shirt made the patter of my heart slow a bit.

"And you, *mijo*, your pop and I are honored by what you've done today."

Javier kissed the back of his mother's left hand. Between anyone else it would have been oddly formal, but I saw the warmth in the gesture.

"Well." Lex let out a long huff. "Are y'all comin' back to the house now or ar—"

Her question was cut off by the wheels of a car skidding to a stop on the curb next to us. We all turned our heads simultaneously to see the door of the sleek white Porsche open and someone step out. "Mornin' folks, a fine day for a weddin' ain't it?"

We stood there, our bodies tense as we said nothing, trying to figure out how to react to the newcomer.

"Well, I'm Carver and this," the passenger side of the car opened, and another person stepped out, "is my brother, Avery."

I'd never seen nor heard from the men before, but I knew exactly who they were in an instant. I could tell by their accents, by the clothes they wore, and by the fact that they carried themselves with an obvious air of superiority. I would have bet my grandmother's house on their last name being Ward. I caught the knowing look in Javier's eyes when I looked up at him.

"You two related to the Wards?" Javier asked. The answer seemed obvious, but we all needed to hear it.

"We are Barrett Ward's sons, yes," Carver said with a grin.

I looked the man up and down. He was a white man of average height with slightly tanned skin and pale-yellow hair. He and his brother had the same pointed nose and deep-set eyes, but Avery was a little taller and had dirty blonde hair.

"Can we help you, son?" Alma called, her voice a little tight.

Carver flashed her a slick grin, his eyes squinting under the harsh sunlight above us. "You know what, ma'am, I think I've found exactly who I was looking for."

"And who might that be?" Javier asked.

In what little time I'd spent in his company, Javier's tone had never strayed past slight annoyance or exasperation. The rumbling strain in his voice was new but not unwelcome given the circumstances.

"The new Mr. and Mrs. Meza, of course," Avery answered.

"You know, I don't think they're the type of people you want to be lookin' for." I smiled, figuring I'd play into their transparent fake-nice routine.

"Oh?" Carver looked over at his brother. "So y'all aren't the ones who scattered like roaches in the light to try to save yourselves from the inevitable then?"

"Nah." Javier was suddenly standing much closer to me. "But we *are* the ones who don't take too kindly to outsiders tryin' to steal what's rightfully ours."

Carver laughed and Avery shrugged. The nonchalance of the action made me furious.

"My daddy doesn't give a shit about what y'all think is rightfully yours." Avery smirked. "He wants what you have— your land and your business—and I promise you he will go through every single one of you backwoods hicks to get it. So, if I were you, I'd pack the fuck up and get gone before shit really gets ugly."

"Before?" I scoffed.

"Oh, that shit was nothing." Carver grinned, alluding to

38

the fact that someone connected to his family had almost killed Bobby Crenshaw. "One dead hick don't mean shit. A couple of no good hick families, however? That's something else entirely."

Javier let out a sharp breath through his nose. Next to me, Clyde made a stifled choking sound.

"Watch yourself now, son," Benicio ground out. "That kind of talk might stand wherever you're from, but up here, we don't let threats like that slide."

He opened his mouth to speak again but stopped when his brother laid a hand on his arm and offered our group another fake smile. "It's all right, Carver," Avery said. "It's time for us to get going anyway."

"Might be best for y'all to keep out of these mountains." I looked at them both. "You can talk as big and bad as you want, but this shit is still ours and there ain't no way in hell we're just going to let y'all come in and take it."

"You can fight all you want, honey." Carver made his way around the car again and opened the driver's side door. "But I'll tell you now, Barrett Ward ain't never been one for losing, and I doubt he's about to start now."

"We'll see." Javier's voice was dark behind a clenched jaw after the squeal of their tires had already signaled their departure.

# CHAPTER 4

JAVIER

The barn our reception took place in had been beautifully decorated. We were using one of the empty ones behind the Hawkins house and a few of my aunts and cousins had put a lot of work into making it nice. It had been cleaned out and filled with all kinds of sparkling lights, tables for guests, and people. I'd hoped the gathering would bring our families together and it looked to be working, but I didn't get the chance to enjoy any of it.

I spotted Adrian, my best friend, cutting up with one of my cousins on the dance floor. He'd traveled hours from a small college town in Eastern Kentucky to celebrate my wedding. He hadn't made it in time for the actual ceremony, and it looked like I wasn't going to get the chance to spend much time with him at the reception.

Me, Hannah, Clyde, and my parents sat huddled around the main table, voices low as we plotted our next course of action. As soon as we'd gotten word a man in the Hawkins camp had almost been murdered, we'd started taking the new threat seriously. Hell, our little gathering was a testament to that. Still, as pressing as the matters were, I'd hoped Hannah and I would at least get a peaceful wedding day before all hell started breaking loose.

Obviously, I'd been wrong.

"Maybe we can ambush them," my mother suggested.

Hannah shook her head. "We don't know where they're stationed yet or what their numbers are."

"Besides," I chimed in. "I don't know if I'm up for any type of ambush that involves more bloodshed."

"Yes." Clyde nodded, looking at me with something akin to approval. "I think it's best if we avoid any more violence, as much as possible. We've been somewhat peaceful for a while now. That's why the rest of the community has put up with us for so long. If we start a war that gets bodies littered through their streets, it won't be a good look for any of us."

Pop hummed and stroked his chin. "You're right. We don't need to invite any more attention to this than necessary. And we don't need any lost lives, on either side."

"So, where does that leave us then?" Mami asked. "They obviously don't care about spilling blood and we do, which gives them the upper hand."

"Not necessarily," Hannah said quietly. "They can try and spill all the blood they want, but his son said they wanted what we had. That can only mean our business, right? They probably want to take our clients away from us, but our clients will never side with them if they create a bloodbath that makes them too dirty to deal with. I think we should start by convincin' those clients it's in their best interests not to bite if the Wards come sniffin' at their doors."

I nodded. "That's a good idea. And not just the big clients but everybody we ever sold as much as a couple of jars to needs to know we're here to stay. We turn the public against them, and it'll be harder for them to push their way past us."

"Exactly." Hannah smiled at me.

I swallowed, harshly, taking a sip of the clear corn liquor in my hand. Having only shine served at our wedding reception was putting it on a little thick, but the Hawkins made a damn good glass of bourbon. That couldn't be denied, no matter how much our families disliked each other.

"So, how are we goin' to do that then?" Clyde asked.

"We'll have some of the more popular members of the families get the word around town." Hannah looked at me. "And my dear new husband and I will take a trip down to Tennessee in a few days to talk with Liza Hayes, our biggest client. After that, we'll go from there."

"Hold up." My drink was suspended halfway up to my mouth. "Y'all sell to Liza Hayes? The same Liza Hayes whose family owns *Bass & Tempo*?"

The place was one of the most famous music venues in the world. Every artist worth their salt who passed through Nashville dreamed of performing there, and the Hayes family had been making or breaking those dreams since it first opened in the '50s.

"The very one." Hannah grinned. "They've got a speakeasy downstairs for their hoity-toity guests, and Liza

JODIE SLAUGHTER

likes to serve out shine to make it a more 'authentic' experience or whatever."

"Well damn." I sat back in my seat. "All right, then."

"I guess that's all we can do for now." Pop sighed, settling back into his chair. He looked tired. Deep lines settled in his forehead and around his mouth. "We're goin' to ramp up security around all the facilities and stash houses."

We all nodded in agreement.

"While we get the word out to our customers, I'll put some people on finding out more about the family," Hannah offered. "Where they operate out of, how many of them they are, stuff like that. We can get together again in a week and a half. Javier and I should be back from our little honeymoon by then."

Hannah was joking. I knew it and everyone else knew it. But the words sent a jolt through me. They reminded me that she and I had gotten married, that I had a wife again. For me, there was a certain pressure that came with that knowledge—a pressure to be a good husband to her, in whatever way that meant for us. I didn't care if we only stayed married for a few weeks or if we never so much as slept in the same bed together. Hannah Hawkins was my wife.

We hadn't gone the sentimental route with our vows, but I knew what the commitment meant to me. She was mine to care for, to look after, to protect, to serve. To do all the things I'd neglected during my first foray into being a husband. I was going to do right by her, so I started by trying to add some resemblance of normalcy to her wedding night.

"Hannah," I said softly, prompting her to look up at me

44

with those big, shining eyes. "Would you do me the honor of dancin' with me?"

The son of one of Hannah's runners was DJ-ing, and he'd done a hell of a job catering to this audience, even down to the slow Gary Clark Jr. song he now had flowing from the speakers.

Hannah's eyes widened for a moment before she accepted my outstretched hand. "Sure."

Nobody paid us a lick of attention as I led her over to the makeshift dance floor. It was the exact opposite of most of the weddings I had been to, but I didn't mind it much. Neither of us had to plaster fake smiles on our faces or get worried about looking like we weren't happy or in love. Everyone there knew our marriage was in name only and there was no expectation for us to present it any differently. It was almost comforting.

"Long day." I breathed in the light traces of perfume she wore. Hannah wasn't short, but her head still didn't reach any taller than my neck.

"As hell. I can't wait to get home and in my damn bed."

"That does sound good."

"What?" Hannah leaned back a bit and smiled up at me. "Bein' in my bed?"

My brain stuttered for a second at the pure mischief in her tone. If she wanted to play, I was more than willing.

"Can't say that sounds too bad at all." I tried to keep my face as straight as possible. "But I meant I can't wait to get comfortable, *wife.*"

She made a little groan. "You goin' to keep calling me that?"

"Probably."

"And if I just start callin' you 'husband' all the time?"

I shrugged as much as I could with her in my arms. She laid her head back on my chest, ear to heart. "It's what I am, ain't it?"

"You mean to tell me it doesn't feel weird as hell? Me callin' you husband?"

"There are much worse things I could be called than your husband, Hannah. Much worse. I can promise you that."

She stilled and then leaned back again, looking up at me with something in her gaze that reminded me of the sun on a hot July afternoon. I hadn't expected my words to cause such a reaction, but I couldn't say I was mad they had.

In a blink, her eyes left mine and her cheek was pressed up against my chest again. Only this time, the hands she had clasped around my neck tightened just a bit.

"Shut up and dance, Javier."

Which I did, leading her for two more songs before we finally separated, the feeling of her soft body gone from mine leaving me a bit colder than before.

I'd accepted Hannah's request to move into the Hawkins house during our negotiations, but I didn't get rid of my house. I didn't know how long our arrangement was going to last, and I didn't want to put the cart before the horse. So I arrived at Hannah's place with only a few duffle bags full of clothes, toiletries, and valuables.

"It's just you here?" I asked as we entered the empty house, wondering about her younger sister.

"Yeah." She flicked on a few lights. "Nicole got her own place a few weeks ago. She said she could feel Mama and Granny watching her every time she so much as took a step in here."

I didn't know how to respond to that, so I didn't.

She took one of my duffles and led me through the hallway and up a set of stairs. "My room is right there." She pointed to a closed door I assumed held the master bedroom. "I'm givin' you my old room. Got a new bed for you and everything."

"That'll be just fine, thank you." I heaved one of my bags onto my shoulder to take some of the weight off my hand.

"There's only one bathroom up here so we'll have to share it unless you feel like goin' downstairs. You don't take long showers, do you?"

"Not really."

"Good, because I do, and I don't want you usin' up all my hot water. These old ass pipes don't make enough."

I snorted and Hannah flashed me a smile.

"Okay, then." She walked towards my room, flicked a light on, and sat the bag on the floor before shuffling back into the doorway. "I'm goin' to bed. Finally."

"Right." I coughed. "Me too."

Hannah stood there, her arms folded on top of her chest. It was probably the only time I'd ever seen her look anything close to awkward. It was cute as all hell.

"I'll call Liza in the morning to tell her we're comin'

down there." She turned abruptly as she crossed the hallway towards her bedroom door.

"Wife," I called out, hoping my voice sounded lighter than I felt.

"What?"

"You look beautiful."

She still had her back to me so I couldn't see her face, but I watched her shoulders loosen just a bit.

"You already told me that this morning."

"Well, they say a man should never take his wife for granted. Especially not his brand new bride."

The soft raspiness of her laughter was infectious, even after she closed the door in my face.

# CHAPTER 5

HANNAH

I unwrapped my hair for no one before eight am, not even on weekdays. So at a little after seven in the morning the day after our wedding, Javier found me in the kitchen with a freshly washed face, ratty pajamas, and my leopard print headscarf.

"Mornin'," he greeted.

I grunted out a response with a mouth full of cereal.

"You got any coffee?"

I shook my head, chewed quickly, and then swallowed. "I don't drink coffee."

Javier's eyes widened as if it was the most ridiculous thing he'd ever heard. "What?"

I rolled my eyes. "It tastes like garbage." I shrugged. "And it's bad for you."

"Jesus Christ, my wife is a blasphemer."

"There's plenty of orange juice in the fridge. Or some unsweetened cranberry juice if you want to take some preventative measures against UTIs."

Javier smacked his lips. "I'll just stick with water."

He grabbed a clean glass from next to the sink, filled it with tap water, and sat down across from me.

The eat-in kitchen table was small, only two chairs, so our arms were close enough to brush up against each other from where they rested on either side of it. The soft, dark hairs that littered his forearms brushed mine and made the fine hairs on my body stand on end.

He stared at me as I ate, those dark eyes all intense and open. I was surprised when his steady gaze didn't make me uncomfortable. I wasn't normally one to squirm under duress, but Javier's eyes had a severity to them I wasn't sure he even realized.

"You hungry? There's plenty of cereal in the cabinet."

I drained my cereal bowl of leftover milk then sat it back down on the table.

"That milk would tear me up," he replied.

"Are you lactose intolerant?"

He nodded.

"Mama was too…"

I trailed off. Most of the time, it still hurt to think about her. Every time I got sad thinking about her favorite movie or the way her voice used to sound echoing through the halls of the house, I felt a little weaker. Like I was going to do exactly the opposite of what she had always taught me and crumble right where I stood.

I had no interest in crumbling in front of Javier, and it wasn't because I didn't trust him. It was because he wasn't family. He was my husband—I had the papers to prove it sitting on the dresser in my room—but he wasn't my family. And I'd be damned if I broke down in front of somebody who wasn't family.

"I'll put some soy milk on the grocery list." I faked a smile. "I don't need any dairy puttin' you out of commission right before we head to Nashville."

"Speaking of." He leaned a little closer to me and I could smell the minty freshness of his breath. "When are we headin' out? Did you talk to Liza Hayes?"

"Sure did." I swallowed and leaned away from him just a bit. I didn't want to lose my train of thought. "First thing this morning. She said she can meet with us tomorrow afternoon."

"That's soon."

Standing up from the table, I grabbed my bowl and went over to the sink to wash it out. We needed a damn dishwasher.

"She's a busy woman." I shrugged. "And we need to get in there as soon as possible so we can get home. I don't want to be away too long with things goin' to hell and all."

He hummed, a deep, rumbly noise of understanding that made my gut clench.

"So we'll leave in the mornin' then?" Javier was suddenly behind me, so close I could smell him. He wore no cologne but his scent was still mouthwatering, all fresh with a slight tinge of clean sweat. The front of his body was pressed slightly up against my back as he placed his empty glass in the sink. I hated how much I enjoyed the feel of him, soft and hard at the same time.

"First light." I hoped he didn't note the shakiness in my voice.

He was gone from me just as quick as he'd come, now leaning with his hip against the counter a couple of feet away from me. "I can drive if you want. It ain't that long a ride."

"A little over four hours. I'll drive us home then."

He smiled and the seizing of my stomach was back again. I needed to leave—leave the room, leave the house. Be as far away from Javier as I could.

"Look at us," he said, fanning the flame that was already building in me. "Compromisin' like a good married couple already."

I didn't grace him with a response before I fled back to the safety of my bedroom.

———

I was up before dawn the next morning getting ready to leave, happy I'd heard Javier up too. It meant I didn't have to see him any sooner than necessary by having to wake him up.

I'd spent pretty much the entire day before avoiding him completely. The first few hours after our kitchen encounter was spent in my bedroom. By early afternoon I'd left the house completely, performing bullshit errands and driving my sister crazy while she looked over our sales numbers. By the time I made it home, it was well past dinner. I felt almost guilty for leaving Javier without a word and forcing him to have his supper alone, but I didn't apologize as I eyed the dim light shining from underneath his bedroom door as I crept in.

I felt like the biggest coward of all time, and I was ashamed of it. It felt like I was admitting defeat, showing that something about Javier Meza made me feel scared and unsure. If she could have seen me, Mama would have flicked me on the ear and told me Hawkins women didn't cower for anybody, especially not in our own damned house.

My teeth clamped together. When thoughts of Mama weren't nearing me to tears, they were giving me the kind of guidance I couldn't get from anyone else, not even myself. I wondered if I'd ever stop feeling the need to fill her shoes so exactly. Honestly, I doubted it.

I jumped a tiny bit in shock when I heard the creaking of footsteps right outside my door. When he didn't continue down the stairs and no-knock came, I wondered what the hell Javier was doing.

"Yes?" I asked as I threw the door open.

"Uh," he coughed a bit, "I just wanted to see if you were ready. Sun's goin' to be up in just a few minutes."

Javier wore dark jeans, a white t-shirt, and a pair of beat-up boots. He looked annoyingly handsome in that simplistic way of his.

"Yeah, I'm ready whenever you are." I flashed him a small smile. "We can get breakfast on the road."

He grabbed my duffle bag and started down the stairs. Within minutes, the house was locked up and we were on the road, heading towards the highway.

Our ride was mostly silent at first, the only sounds being the soft music I played from the speakers of Javier's SUV. It wasn't the type of awkward silence that always happened when you were stuck in a confined space with someone you barely knew. Instead, it was surprisingly comfortable. Javier didn't even voice any complaints as I propped my bare feet up on his dashboard.

The ride was smooth and the visual of healthy green trees and dark highway pavement even helped me doze off a few times.

It wasn't until we stopped at a drive-thru in London, Kentucky for breakfast an hour and a half later that the conversation picked up.

"So, how did your family get hooked up with the Hayeses?" He drove with one hand at the bottom of the wheel and the other clutching a sausage biscuit.

"Mama lived in Nashville for a little while when she was younger." I took a long sip of my orange juice. "She tended bar at the speakeasy." I snorted. The visual never failed to put a smile on my face. "Her and Liza were friends."

Javier made a noise of acknowledgment. "That's a hell of a connection."

"I'm sure y'all have some too."

The Mezas hadn't become our rivals because they only hawked shine to local teenagers and bars. I knew they had just as far a reach as we did.

He took his eyes off the road ahead for a split second just to flash me a grin. Those white teeth against the darkness of his beard made a beautiful contrast, so much that I had to look down at my bare thighs and pick at the frayed edges of my denim shorts.

"A few." His voice was full of false nonchalance. "Everybody on Millionaire's Row during Derby weekend always seems to find themselves with plenty of Meza liquor on hand."

Now *that* was shocking. I didn't even bother to keep the impressed look off my face. The tourists loved to sip on Mint Juleps made with shitty mixers, but anybody looking for a true Kentucky experience wanted something less sweet and watered down. Apparently, that thing was Meza moonshine.

"How did you make that happen?" I asked.

"Same as y'all did. Mami knew the right people and made a deal."

"To our mamas then." I raised my cup of orange juice in a toast. "For always gettin' shit done."

"Absolutely. Our families would be nothin' without them."

It was another three hours before we got to Nashville. By the time we made it downtown to Music Row, the streets were already full of people. *Bass & Tempo* sat in the middle of it all, the large, dark building right between a honky-tonk and a BBQ spot. Our hotel was across the way and down the street a little, some semi-gentrified "boutique" hotel with less than twenty-five rooms. It had also been expensive as hell. The cost of Javier and I staying for one night probably could have paid for almost a week's stay at the one bed and breakfast we had in Harlan.

Making moonshine had made my family incredibly comfortable, but it hadn't made us rich, and certainly not wealthy. Both the Hawkins and Meza families put what extra money we had after taking care of ourselves and our people back into our communities.

I didn't care how comfortable the hotel's beds were or how pretty the marble tile in the bathroom was, the only reason we were staying there was that it was close to the venue. I knew we both would have been perfectly fine staying at some chain hotel if it was clean and relatively comfortable otherwise.

"Mornin'," I greeted the front desk attendant and handed over my ID as Javier stood next to me. "I should have a reservation under Hawkins. I called ahead for early check-in."

"Hannah?" he said, eyes on his computer screen.

"Yes."

"All right, I have you down for a corner room with a queen-sized bed."

"What? No," I sputtered. "I booked a room with two double beds."

I reached in my purse for my phone and quickly pulled up my confirmation email. "See?" I held the screen up to him. "Two double beds, says so right there."

I was sure my voice was inching closer towards panicked and to his credit, the attendant maintained his patience.

"Yes ma'am, but when you requested early check-in service, we were forced to make other accommodations for you. We don't have any double bedrooms available currently."

"Well, we can wait. We can come back when the people in it now are checked out."

He shook his head. "I apologize, ma'am, but it's already

been booked. We can give you a partial refund if you'd like to cancel your reservation."

"Partial?" My eyes widened.

Suddenly, I felt Javier's warm hand on my shoulder. The front of his body was pressed up against me again. "The queen bed will be fine," he said.

His tone was soft, and I wasn't sure whether he was speaking to me or the front desk attendant. Either way, it calmed me, but only a little. We didn't have the time to find another hotel. I also didn't want the money we'd already spent to go to waste. I was going to have to suck it the fuck up and share a bed with my husband, even if the thought of it scared me out of my damn mind.

I swallowed...then made up my mind. We would take the room, but I still hoped like hell they had some sort of mini couch one of us could sleep on.

They didn't.

The hotel was small, and our room was even smaller. There was only one little dresser topped with a television and two nightstands on both sides of the bed. That damned bed. The longer I stared at it, the smaller it looked. My tunnel vision made me wonder if we were going to have to sleep on top of each other at the end of the night.

Jesus.

The fucking thought of that made sweat bead up on the back of my neck.

"It's hot as all hell in here," Javier said, voicing my thoughts.

I didn't say a word as I turned around and adjusted the thermostat, listening for the air conditioner to kick on.

"It'll cool down in a minute."

The words were filled with more hope than comfort.

"What time do we need to meet with Liza?" He was shuffling through his bag for something.

I looked at the time on my phone. "Eleven-thirty. We should probably go ahead and wash up."

Javier extended an arm towards the bathroom. "You can go ahead first."

Neither of us mentioned the glaring, queen-sized elephant standing in the middle of the room. Not as I washed up and changed my clothes, not when Javier did the same, and definitely not when we finally headed out.

# CHAPTER 6

HANNAH

*Bass & Tempo* wasn't a huge place. Placed on a street already packed with connected buildings, it was taller than it was wide. The inside had floors made of some kind of dark wood and two levels with balconies above the ground floor. The stage definitely wasn't one you'd find in some large stadium, but even empty it held a certain power. I had no musical talent to speak of, but even I had a brief desire to stand up on it.

One of Liza's upstairs bartenders escorted Javier and me to her office in the back of the house. It was small and smelled like cigarettes but was still tidy.

Her hazel eyes lit up as soon as she saw me. Liza was a short, thin woman in her sixties with golden brown skin and a head full of loose, light brown curls. The closer she got to me, the clearer the dark freckles that dotted her nose became.

"Hannah-girl." She wrapped her arms around me. "It's so good to see you again."

Liza had come to my mother's funeral but I hadn't gotten much of a chance to talk with her. Outside of my grief, I'd been busy making sure everything ran smoothly as dozens of people shuffled in and out of the church and then my house to pay their respects. If Liza had tried to make actual conversation with me that day, I probably would have been too shut down to remember it.

"It's good to see you too, Miss Liza. Thank you for takin' the time to see me again."

"Uh-huh." We separated, her eyes no longer on my face but behind me. "So this is him, then?"

Javier offered her a handshake. "Javier Meza, and it's a pleasure to meet you, ma'am."

"Mmmhmm." She looked him up and down. "You're a handsome thing, ain't you?"

Javier didn't answer, but he tilted the baseball cap on his head back a bit and flashed her a sly smile.

Liza's eyes widened. "As far as husbands go, you could have done worse, Hannah-girl." She made her way to the side of her desk, sitting on top. Javier and I parked ourselves in the chairs on the other side. "Not that I'd know first-hand, mind you, but still, this one is *fine*."

Liza had never wanted to get married, but she and her boyfriend had been together for nearly thirty years. They had two sons together, one who traveled while working as a sound engineer for touring musicians, and the other who helped Liza run the family business in Nashville.

I didn't know what to say to her words. I had no clue which one of us she was complimenting. It wasn't like I'd really put a ton of thought into the man's looks before I'd agreed to marry him. Of course, knowing how handsome he was had made the decision a little easier to deal with, but still.

"So," Liza cleared her throat, her face suddenly all business, "what is it exactly y'all wanted to talk about? I don't think I got a clear understandin' on our call."

In an instant, I felt like a child in the middle of some play, pretend game. Our meeting wasn't formal, but I'd worn a nice dress and a pair of heeled sandals. I'd been trying to go for a look of professionalism, but I had also been trying to play a part. One of a leader who had her shit together even when the reality was the exact opposite.

"Well," I sat forward in my seat, "I know you have a longstandin' deal with my family. We swing cases of our shine every month for your speakeasy and you pay us well for that. It's been going on for over twenty years, but I just wanted to meet with you and make sure we were still solid."

Her eyebrows furrowed. "Why wouldn't we be?"

When I opened my mouth but didn't answer immediately, she pressed even more.

"Is there somethin' I don't know about? Maybe somethin' to do with the reason you brought your strappin' new husband along to this meetin' with you?"

"We're in danger, Liza," I said.

"Danger? I thought the local sheriff's office left y'all alone up there."

I shook my head and spared a look at Javier. He was sitting forward too, his mouth tightly closed like he wanted to speak but was holding himself back.

"It ain't the cops. It's someone else." A long sigh left me.

"Some rich family from Lexington. They're tryin' to steal everything my family has worked for." I nodded to Javier. "His too. We're just here to make sure we can still count on your business even while things are shaky."

Liza had been close with my mother and for that reason alone, I loved and respected her. But I had no interest in laying all my business out there. She didn't need to know about the truth of my new marriage or the fact that our families might be close to starting a war that could turn out to be brutal.

"Ma'am," Javier started. "I'm sure you know how hard Miss Joy worked to keep her family business strong. And you may not know me or my name, but my family has done the same thing. Both of us, the Hawkins and the Mezas. We fought for our place, had people die for our right to just exist up in them mountains. The rest of the country may have forgotten about that, but we haven't."

I could see him looking up at her with those eyes, so earnest they bordered on hypnotic. Miss Liza was enraptured by his words, and I was too.

"We're goin' to make sure they don't accomplish what they're tryin' to do, but we need to make sure the people who have always been with us are still with us while we do that."

Liza was silent for a few moments, looking at him with her thin lips clamped shut. Then, she turned to me.

"So that's why you brought him then?" She smirked. "I think that man could probably convince me to take my clothes off and run naked through the damn streets if he turned them eyes on me for long enough."

"Yeah." I coughed. "He has a way with words."

"Hannah-girl." Liza quickly turned serious and reached over the table to lay a warm hand against my cheek. "I'd let every cabinet in that waterin' hole downstairs run dry before I betrayed your mama. Dead or alive, Joy Hawkins would beat my ass if I even thought about doin' that shit."

"Thank you, Miss Liza." I smiled, feeling as light as a feather. "Thank you."

She clapped her hands together once and stood up. "Well, now that business is all taken care of, why don't y'all come downstairs tonight? Our headliner has agreed to play a few songs for the folks in the speakeasy. It'll be fun. Then tomorrow, we can renegotiate the terms of that deal of ours. Business has been pickin' up lately, and I think we're goin' to need a few more cases a month."

I stood with her, trying like hell to rein in my growing excitement. "Sounds like a deal, Miss Liza."

"All right then, y'all get on now. I've got some real work to do." She winked.

We exchanged handshakes by the door, and when she went to shake Javier's hand, he clasped both of his around hers. "I want to thank you for today, ma'am. I know your promise means a lot to my wife, so it means a lot to me too."

He sounded sincere, painfully so, and that gave me pause.

"Well, as I said, I'd do just about anything for Joy. Especially somethin' as easy as this. Now," she all but closed the door in our faces, "get on, like I told you. I'll see you at midnight."

By the time we got back to the hotel room after a quick

lunch at the BBQ spot next to *Bass & Tempo*, I could tell Javier was just as exhausted as I was. His broad shoulders sagged a bit and his eyelids looked heavy.

He grabbed his duffle and headed to the bathroom. I was left in the room to stare at that damn bed. It was the same size as the one I had at home, which I'd always found to be pretty big, but at the moment, I wondered how Javier and I could possibly fit together on it. I wasn't a small woman and Javier wasn't exactly little. I hoped we could somehow manage it without falling all over each other and making things more awkward than they already were.

We had no other choice, though. There was no way in hell I was sleeping on the floor, and I wasn't about to be the asshole who made him do it, either.

I refused to get in the bed in my outside clothes, even if it was just for a nap. While Javier was in the bathroom, I changed out of my dress and into a pair of sweatpants and a tank top. My hair was quickly wrapped and secured under a scarf, and I lay on the left side of the bed looking at the most recent picture Nicole had posted on social media.

He paused when he finally left the bathroom. He'd changed out of his clothes too and was wearing a pair of light grey sweats and a t-shirt. I forced myself to keep my eyes on his face. I was already a bit anxious, and I had no idea what the hell I would do if I came face to face with the sight of dick in his sweats.

"Uhm," he ran a hand through his hair, "I guess I'll just…"

I rolled my eyes, my confidence totally fake. "Don't be

goofy, Javier. Just get in the damn bed."

"Are you sure?"

He looked surprised I'd made the suggestion. I wondered if he thought I was planning to make him sleep out in the hallway.

"What kind of married couple would we be if we couldn't even stand to share a bed for a couple nights?" I patted the space next to me. "I just hope you like the right side."

Well," he went over to his side and pulled the covers back, "I normally prefer the left actually, but I guess this will do."

"What was that you were sayin' about compromise earlier?" I joked. "Be a good little husband and take what I've left you."

Javier groaned and grumbled softly but did as instructed.

Our nap lasted longer than both of us intended. As soon as Javier climbed in bed, we fell asleep. One of the alarms I'd set had been completely slept through, and I woke up first at six pm. The first thing I noticed was the sun beating in harshly through the opened curtains. The second was Javier's body against mine.

It was the second time in as many days I'd found him pressed up against my back. This time, his weighty arm had found itself around my waist too. I could feel his breath against the back of my neck. One of his legs folded over my calf.

My body felt like it was on fire. From the apples of my cheeks to the soles of my feet, every inch of him that touched me made my body buzz. He wasn't clutching at me, which made it easy to slip away from him without a problem. But, I didn't. I just lay there, biting down on my lip while being hot and frozen solid at the same time.

I shifted a bit, not entirely sure if I was trying to move farther or closer, but as my ass touched his thighs, I felt another part of him. Just as heavy as the arm he had around me, and hotter by far, his dick had clearly woken up before him. My mouth went dry and my stomach dropped. Javier was still sleeping, so I was sure he had no idea how his body was reacting. I also had no way of knowing if it was a response to me specifically. That didn't stop me from imagining that it was.

What if he was dreaming about me? What if the feeling of my body against his had gotten him so worked up his body couldn't help but get hard at the sensation? It had been months since I'd been so close to anyone in any way that wasn't strictly platonic, and my body didn't know how to react. I became hot between my thighs, pulsing and wetting as I did everything in my power not to push back against him.

In his sleep, the arm Javier had around my waist moved forward and down until it was settled over the pooch of my lower belly. He was so close to where I really wanted him, and I wondered if he could feel the heat coming off my pussy in waves. I swallowed harshly when the breaths on the back of my neck stopped for a second, and then deepened. Then, I felt his eyes. Javier was awake, which meant he was fully aware of the dick he had pressed up against me.

Neither of us said anything for a few seconds, both breathing hard.

"You up?" He was the first to speak.

"Yeah," I answered, my voice still thick from our long sleep.

"Are you feeling okay?" The question was completely out of the blue and wouldn't have felt completely random if I didn't know exactly what he was asking me.

My voice was a whisper. "I feel good."

"Yeah you do." His breath tickled my ear. "Good as hell."

Javier's thumb brushed at the bare skin under my ridden-up shirt. His hand moved lower, slowly. By the time he brushed against the edge of my panties, I was biting down on my lip to keep from moaning. His movements were still hesitant, and I shifted my hips forward some, giving him a nonverbal go-ahead.

This was a bad idea for more reasons than I could recall in the moment. But the logical part of me was completely drowned out by the part that was worked up and screaming for some kind of release. I didn't know what Javier was thinking, but his hardness was full-on pressed against my ass and his hips moved delicately against me, obviously searching for his own.

When he finally dipped his fingers beneath my clothes and into the curls that rested on my mons, I let out a long, shaky breath. Rough, warm fingers traced the seam of my pussy lips and my teeth clamped together. The first touch on my clit had me moaning out loud and sent one of my hands clutching at the forearm he still had around me.

He circled my button round and round and my hips moved in tandem, chasing my own pleasure and making sure to push myself up against his length as well.

"Jesus Christ you're wet," Javier groaned. "Did you wake up like this, or has this pussy been ready for me all this time?"

I shook my head. "I felt you up against me and—"

I stopped myself, not really knowing what to say, and not wanting to put my attention on anything other than his fingers and his cock.

I ground my hips back even harder, dirtier, and smiled in satisfaction once I felt him shudder. Javier's fingers left me and went to my thigh, hooking it over his before he went back inside my underwear. It would have been so easy for him to thrust himself inside of me in this position. The only thing keeping us from connecting fully was our clothes and those could be handled easily and with a quickness…

The second his digits strayed, pressing against my entrance, my second alarm went off. The shrill sound of it was enough to make both of us jump in shock…and bring us back to reality.

"Shit," he muttered behind me and moments later, he'd backed off of me completely.

My breaths were still deep, and my cunt was still aching, now even more eager to be filled and played with. How had we allowed something like this to happen? I decided to chalk it up to our long sleep completely fucking with our minds and our sense of reason.

"It's fine, Javier." I bit down on my bottom lip again. "It's fine. Nothing happened. It's fine."

I felt raw and open when I finally looked over at him. I couldn't determine exactly what the look was behind his eyes, but it made my need to get things back to normal even more intense.

"It's fine. Forget about it." I patted his arm. He raised it and I slid out of bed. My tank top had ridden up, so I knew he could see the soft flesh of my stomach. I didn't bother to cover myself.

"You want to go somewhere for dinner?" I asked, rooting through my toiletries bag. "That nap made me hungry as hell."

I didn't want to have any kind of long, in-depth talk about what had happened. I figured, if both of us could ignore it completely, we could pretend like it hadn't happened.

Javier was sitting up against the headboard. His shirt had ridden up too and the dips of muscle in his hips made my eyes widen. Thankfully, it seemed like he was just as fine with playing into the ruse as I was.

"Yeah," he said quietly. "We should get some hot chicken."

"You're goin' to eat hot chicken even when you can't drink any milk to stop your mouth from burnin' all to hell?"

He looked almost offended at the suggestion. "I'm a pro at hot chicken, wife." He smiled, but it was strained. "Ain't no spice in the world hot enough to take me out."

"Uh-huh. I guess we'll see."

Javier was right. He sweated a little when he bit into the hot chicken thigh he'd ordered, but he handled the heat like a pro. I, on the other hand, ordered a mild recipe and felt my tongue grow numb almost instantly. Javier snickered when I refused to admit defeat, even as my eyes started watering.

The rest of the day was spent killing time and patently not talking about what we'd almost done. We visited the park near Music Row for a little while, checked out a record store close to our hotel and an open mic night before quickly dipping out because of the awful singing. I started getting ready as soon as we got back to the hotel room, showering and pinning my hair up into a Goddess braid. By the time Javier stepped out of his own shower, fully dressed in an outfit similar to the one he'd had on earlier that day—only this time with a black button-up shirt, a pair of black cowboy boots, and a wide-brimmed cowboy hat—I was ready too.

I had on a dress again, but it was short, tighter, and darker than the one I'd had on in our meeting with Liza. I'd packed it on impulse but was happy as hell I'd done it.

Javier let out a long, low whistle when he saw me, wiggling his eyebrows in a silly manner.

"I look good, huh?" I asked.

"You're goin' to light that room on fire the second you step in it, woman." He placed a hand over his heart.

"You are so damn corny!"

"I'm not corny. I'm honest."

"Corny," I coughed.

Javier's laughter made me smile.

"You ready?" It was already a little after midnight and I was surprisingly excited to see what the speakeasy looked like. I pictured someplace dark and smoky and filled with people drunk on the knowledge they were doing something sexy and illegal.

"Whenever you are, wife."

# CHAPTER 7

JAVIER

I had no idea what I'd been expecting Liza's speakeasy to look like, but I was surprised the second we stepped inside. Upstairs, Bass & Tempo was simplistic and unassuming. It was nice but also obvious the venue made no attempts to show up the artists who performed there. Downstairs was an entirely different story. The walls were covered in some kind of emerald green velvet and the floors were pristine black and white subway tiles. A small stage sat against the far wall and a long bar took up a considerable amount of the right side of the room.

Bodies filled the space from wall to wall. Some people were at the bar, some were sitting at the little black tables, and others were gathered in front of the empty stage.

Liza had put our names on whatever list the bouncer behind the thick black basement door had so we'd been let inside without any fuss. But neither Hannah or I seemed to know what to do.

"Damn." Hannah whistled lowly.

"I know," I said. "This is—"

"Cool as hell."

"Thank you." We both turned to see Liza standing behind us with a smile on her face. "I'm proud of my little project."

"You should be." Hannah's tone was dripped in honesty. "It's incredible in here."

Liza just smiled again. "Well, I apologize I don't have time to shoot the shit with y'all tonight but a boss' work is never done. Drink, enjoy the show, have fun."

That was all she left us with before she disappeared into the crowd the same way she'd come.

"Let's get a table," Hannah suggested, already heading towards an open one on the left wall.

I trailed her, not touching but close enough that I didn't lose her in the swarm of people. I let Hannah sit then excused myself to get us drinks. When I came back with two glasses of Hawkins bourbon, she smiled widely.

"Hmmm." Her full lips were clamped and pursed when she made the noise.

"What?" I said in a mock defensive tone.

"Nothin', nothin'. It's just," she paused to take a sip, "this is the second time I've seen you choose some Hawkins shine even when you could have gotten somethin' else."

"I'm here to support you, remember? How would it look if I was drinkin' anythin' else? We need to present a united front, wife."

Hannah didn't say anything, but she made that noise again.

"And don't think I didn't see you sippin' on a glass of

Meza's finest at our reception either," I continued, refusing to take my eyes off hers.

She looked down and picked at her white painted finger-nails. "Well, bitter rivals or not, y'all know how to cook up a good glass of gin."

I couldn't help but puff my chest out a little at her compliment. "Oh, you liked that, huh?"

Her eyes narrowed a little, but I didn't let it stop my joking.

"I'm glad you did. I spent months comin' up with that recipe."

"Hold up." She looked almost impressed. "You came up with that recipe?"

"Sure did. Decided to make our base mash out of pineapples instead of corn. We distilled it four different times so that flavor really came through."

Most people assumed the term "corn liquor" was just some kind of goofy saying, but it wasn't. The most basic kind of moonshine was made by mixing up a heap of cornmeal with water and sugar and yeast and letting it ferment until it was good and ready to be distilled and turned into liquor. Gin, bourbon, and vodka all started with the same kinds of ingredients. It was up to the shine maker to perfect the things like taste and proof and fusions. I'd always looked at it as an art form.

"So, you actually get out there with the cookers and make shine then?" Hannah seemed shocked.

"Since I was a boy." I smiled at the memories of myself running barefoot through kitchens and cooking spots, trying my damndest to get a peek at what was going on. "Pop tried like hell to keep me away from it, but I wouldn't give. You were never interested?"

Hannah shrugged. "I don't know. Mama always told me that my job was to run the business and that we hired people to make the shine so we could focus on the other parts. I check out the kitchens regularly and taste the product but that's about it. "

"That's what Pop always said too. That man spent years tryin' to fashion me into a leader before he finally gave up."

Every time I thought about it, my spirit darkened. Hannah, my wife of two days, seemed to sense the change in my mood easier than my own father did.

"You didn't want to lead your people?" She asked the question with a certain hesitation, like she was scared I'd blow up instead of answering her.

"Nah." I shook my head. "I ain't never seen myself as much of a leader. I like to work with my hands, not have anybody answerin' to me. Besides, I don't think I'm the kind of person who inspires loyalty in people. Not like you."

Hannah snorted then took a large gulp of her clear bourbon. "I've only been the boss for a few months. I don't know what kind of loyalty I could possibly be inspirin' in my people."

Without thinking much on it, I reached across the table and laid my hand on top of hers. Hannah's skin was soft and warm, and I was thankful as hell she didn't reject my touch.

"The fact that they're still with you shows that. Shit, we may be all about tradition but ain't no way we're stickin' around and takin' orders from somebody we can't stand. Both of our families have had enough of that shit to last a lifetime."

Hannah smiled and tucked a piece of her hair behind her ear. It was probably the first time I'd seen her show anything close to bashfulness. There was a vulnerability to it I hadn't experienced with her and it made me want to be closer to her, to touch her. I didn't want to be a creep and get up in her space without permission, but I did rub the pad of my thumb against the back of her hand. The wide-eyed look she shot me in response made me want to keep up the motion forever.

We just sat there quietly for a while, staring silently at one another until a bit of feedback sounded through the microphone on the stage. Finally taking my hand from hers, I turned to see a young white woman with pink hair cut close to her head in a white jumpsuit. Within seconds, a small three-person band filed onto the stage behind her. It took them next to no time to set up, and after a brief introduction, she began her first song.

Her voice wasn't what I would describe as soulful, but it was still beautiful. Soft and a little haunting, backed by a low, grinding beat that instantly made me nod my head. Her first song was short, barely a couple of minutes, but by the time she started her second song, people had already started filling the dance floor.

I turned back to Hannah to see her nodding along.

"You want to?" I jerked my head towards the crowd at the front of the room.

She didn't give me a verbal answer, but she did rise out of

her seat, take my hand, and lead me further into the crowd until we were in the center. Bodies moved all around us, some on beat and some off as they swayed and bent and grinded. No one paid any attention to Hannah and me.

I went to wrap my arms around her waist as I'd done during our dance at our reception, but she shook her head at me.

"Uh-uh, this ain't that kind of song, Javier." She walked closer to me, turned, and backed her body up close to me. "Here." I could hear the smile in her voice. "Since you seem to like bein' behind me so damn much."

The people around us faded from my mind completely the second Hannah started to move. She swayed her hips. Wide and full, they moved against me in a way that made me lose my breath. I wrapped an arm around her waist, not just as an excuse to touch her but to steady myself as well. The beat thumped and she moved right along with it. I couldn't do shit but follow along while I tried to keep up with her, show her that no matter what she might have thought, I had no problem handling her.

One song turned into two, then three, both of us moving and dipping and rubbing up against each other. The room got progressively hotter, I could feel the heat radiating through Hannah's clothes, and a light sheen of sweat glossed over my forehead and the back of my neck.

The slow beat turned into one that was faster and headier. Hannah dipped at the waist a bit, not bending much, but low enough that I could make out the sexy ass arch in her back. My arms strayed from around her waist to rest on her hips, my own hips moving in tandem with hers as she grinded against me.

Hannah's arch straightened but instead of going back to her earlier position, she got closer to me. I thought back to the way I'd woken up that morning, her lush ass pressed up against my crotch and her scent surrounding me. Just like that time spent in bed, her soft body on mine set me on fire.

Hannah leaned her head back against my shoulder and looked up at me. I knew she couldn't have possibly been drunk or high, but her eyelids looked heavy. I was powerless to do anything but stare back at her as we moved. She had officially seized all my thoughts and actions, claimed them as her own.

I could have stood my ass there forever, in that music-filled club with the taste of bourbon on my lips and the feel of my wife in my arms. But too soon, the musicians set was over. Hannah pulled away first, but not before the singer left the stage and the band started taking their instruments down.

I looked around the room for the first time in a long time. The lights were still dim and instead of live music, sounds flowed through the speakers. The heady energy that had been present thanks to the performer was disappearing, but there was still a haze of lust throughout the space. My wristwatch told me it was nearing three am. We hadn't talked about how long we'd stay, but our time in Liza's speakeasy felt like it had been much shorter than three hours.

Even with the long nap we'd taken earlier in the day, I was starting to feel tired again. My normal sleep schedule had me in bed by eleven and up at six. The past few days had completely fucked that up. Luckily, when I looked down at Hannah, she looked eager to leave too.

"You ready to go on back?"

We'd just been all over each other, but it was the first time I'd opened my mouth to speak in a while.

"Yeah, sure," she answered softly.

I prompted her to move in front of me to walk, noticing the slight shake her legs made with the first couple of steps.

"Hey." I reached out to lay a hand on her bare shoulder. "You all right?"

When Hannah turned, she had a slight grimace on her face. "My feet just hurt. I'm not really used to bein' in heels for this long. I'll be okay though. The walk back to the hotel ain't that far."

At our wedding, she'd worn a pair of low-heeled sandals. By the time the reception had rolled around, she'd been in flats. Sexy as they were, I definitely didn't envy the fact that her feet had to be strapped into those painful-looking things.

"How about I carry you?"

Hannah looked surprised at the suggestion and for a second, I was scared I'd been too forward. Then, she smiled.

"Uh, if you're sure you can—"

"Please." I rolled my eyes. "That ain't no damn problem, I promise you." I turned my back to her. "Now hop on, wife."

I heard her grumble for a second before I felt her weight. She was soft even as her thighs wrapped tightly around me and her arms gripped my chest.

"Damn," Hannah breathed in my ear as we finally exited

the speakeasy. "I see why you like bein' behind me so much now. This shit is fun as fuck."

I barked out a laugh. "Well, next time, you can carry me on your back then, so I can get the full experience."

Hannah's thick thighs tightened around me as I stepped off of the curb and into the street.

"Nah, my back definitely ain't as strong as yours, husband."

The word made me shiver, and by the pleased humming noise she let off in my ear, Hannah felt it run through me.

# CHAPTER 8

HANNAH

Making moonshine was an involved process, especially when you made as much as we did. Usually, we started with a base mash. Something simple but strong. We made them multiple batches at a time using huge barrels to ferment for about two weeks before the corn liquor was ready to be distilled. The distilling process was what turned the mash into drinkable liquor. While the general steps were the same, they tended to differ based on what type of liquor we were trying to make.

The Hawkins had made our name on my great granddaddy's bourbon recipe, and it was still our top seller. Our gin was a close second. Under Mama's guidance, the family had branched out more, started using fruit mashes to make brandy and flavored vodka.

I'd admitted to Javier I only really knew the basics of making shine, and I hadn't been lying. But, as a leader, I still had duties to attend to, duties that involved me pretending like I knew what the hell my cooks were talking about anytime I had to visit the kitchens.

Javier and I had returned from Nashville with an agreement to double Liza Hayes' monthly shipment. We'd planned to meet with his parents about our next steps, but they'd decided to take a trip of their own, apparently visiting whoever it was that had helped make that Millionaire's Row setup happen. So, three days after we returned, after renewing handshake deals with every bar owner in Harlan, I was forced to take a trip to Lynch, Kentucky. Black Mountain, the place where we kept our kitchens.

The mountain was big, the highest peak in the state of Kentucky. It was more than twenty-five hundred feet from top to bottom. It was covered in a thick brush of tall trees and dark wooded areas that made it easy to stay private. Hikers flocked from all over the country, but they tended to stay on the paved roads and trails.

Lynch had a population of under a thousand people, the majority of them descendants of the small number of people who'd stayed even after the coal jobs left. I wouldn't say the locals loved us—because they absolutely didn't—but they and their cops tolerated us working on their mountain so long as we kept a light footprint, stayed out of trouble, and kept the one bar in town stocked with whiskey. It was a fine deal, one that was crucial to making sure our operation stayed up and running the way it always had.

There was a mountain closer to home in Harlan—Pine Mountain. One that would have been a perfectly fine place for our distillers if the forest wasn't classified as a nature preserve which made it a high traffic area. The hour between Lynch and Harlan also served to make it harder for anybody to connect my family name to the setup if an outsider caught wind of our presence up there.

We kept our presence on Black Mountain in two different areas stationed a couple of miles apart. One area held the kitchens where we experimented, made our base mashes, and stored our barrels for fermenting. The other area held the stills, the place where we turned those mashes into liquor and bottled it up for distribution.

My trip had me hiking through the brush of grass and trees into the elevated distilling area. We had six different sixteen-gallon copper stills, all hooked up to gas-powered generators that kept them working on the wooden platforms we'd built to hold them up.

When I was a kid, I thought they were huge, way taller than me and even wider still. I was fresh into my pre-teens when Mama took Nicole and me on a tour at a big-name bourbon distillery in Louisville. When I saw the size of their stills, I lost my breath. Each one of them took up more space than the size of my childhood bedroom, and the sound of them working was so loud I was scared it was going to burst my eardrums. Nicole had found it cool, but I'd been immediately confronted with the fact that our operation was a small one. While Hawkins was a big name in our part of the world, it meant nothing everywhere else, especially when compared to the one on the bottles that distillery had sent out.

Mama must have caught the look on my face, sussed out my expression, and seen it exactly as what it was—fear and embarrassment. She'd run a hand down the back of my head and said nothing, letting us finish the tour. Afterward, we got ice cream, and while Nicole and I enjoyed our cones, she finally started her lecture. I could remember her voice clear as day, all strong and defiant the way it always was when she talked about the family business.

Mama told us it didn't matter how much money we brought in every year, didn't matter that we didn't have fancy bottles filled with over-hyped liquor, and it didn't matter that very few people would ever know who we were. To my mother, only one thing mattered—our family had persisted against all odds.

The prohibition was one among many dark stains on American history, but it had provided us with an opportunity. The Hawkins had been making corn liquor for personal use for decades, and my folks had no intention of stopping because of some horseshit law. Life went on as normal for my folks, but my great granddaddy Wilson saw an opening, one that afforded him a better living than mining coal, and one that upped his standing in the community. He used that to make sure his family was taken care of first. Then, he made a point to hire other black folks in our community, something that would persist so long as I had air in my lungs.

There was a time when just about every black family in Harlan had somebody working for the Hawkins, back when they were still fashioning stills out of pipes and water jugs. Mama made it clear that if we didn't understand enough to be proud of our product yet, we could still find pride in the little pocket of success we'd achieved for our people. No matter how small it might have seemed to others.

Her lecture didn't cow me, but it did open my eyes, made

me a little more accepting of the lessons on leading my mother was always giving me. I may not have expected to be thrust into the position so soon, and definitely not without Mama there to keep guiding me, but I'd long accepted that my time would come someday.

For all my aching and anxiety about the difficulties that came with leading, I was positive none of that other shit was as hard as hiking up a damn mountain on a hot spring morning.

By the time Clyde and I got to our destination, the insides of my thighs had already started to chafe. We were greeted with smiles and hugs by Donna, a short, stout woman with umber skin and incredibly defined cheekbones.

"Mornin' Miss Hannah," she said with her hands at her side. "Clyde."

I wasn't sure I'd ever get used to being referred to with a "Miss" in front of my name, but I considered it a win she didn't call me "Miss Hawkins."

Donna started ahead of us, leading Clyde and me towards the well-maintained wooden building that held our stills.

"Everythin's goin' just fine, Miss Hannah. We got your word about pushin' out three more batches a month and the boys and I won't have no problems gettin' that done."

"That's great to hear, Donna, thank you." I smiled at the three other men in the building. We had more people working in the kitchens, but the stilling process required a little more finesse. The stillers had to know not only how to work the machines, but how to understand the delicate process of distilling different liquors. Donna was in charge, but the three men who worked under her were just as talented. It was why they were the only ones allowed in the stilling house aside from me and Clyde.

The building was hot, even warmer than outside. The ventilation system wasn't bad, but it mostly worked to keep the stills from overheating. I noticed they weren't fussing over it, but Donna and her guys all had a healthy sheen of sweat on their faces. I made a mental note to look into getting them some kind of cooling system. We might not have had the power to install an air conditioner, but I was willing to splurge on a few of those fancy-ass rotating fans.

Donna cleared her throat and then approached me again. While the pride she had in her operation was still clear on her face, there was some hesitancy there too.

"There's just one thing." She gestured for me to follow as she walked over to the last of the six stills in the room. "This one, we call Bess." She lovingly patted the copper machine. "She started actin' up a few weeks ago, wasn't makin' much of anythin' out of the mash we put in her. At first, we thought we were runnin' her too hot, but that wasn't it. Then we figured somethin' was wrong with the tower, but that looks to be just fine too. We think the gas burner is broke, which means the whole damn thing is done 'til we get it fixed."

"Well, is there anything we can do to fix it?"

One of Donna's men shook his head. "Ma'am, that still is nearin' twenty years old. By the time you get your hands on the part and find somebody who knows how to fix it, you'll have spent a damn arm and a leg."

I looked over at Clyde and he stared back.

"Looks like we'll just have to get a new one then," I told him.

"We'll have to make a trip." Clyde's fingers framed his chin. "Maybe go all the way to Louisville. I know a man in the city who might be able to give us a deal."

"What are we lookin' at?"

Not buying the new still wasn't really an option. We needed it, especially now that we needed to make more product. I was already facing a threat from the outside. I didn't need the operation falling apart too. Still, I wanted to know how much it was going to cost me.

"Close to four thousand," he said softly.

I sighed, looking over at the gang of stillers waiting silently. "Well, I guess y'all are gettin' a new still then."

Anyone looking in from the outside would have thought I'd just told them they'd won the lottery with the way they hooted and hollered. I wasn't necessarily excited about the amount of money that needed to be spent, but their enthusiasm was infectious. I couldn't help but smile along with them.

"You think you guys can hold out just a little bit?" I asked, knowing my schedule was full for the next few days. I had a meeting with the Mezas, and then one with some of my own guys. Louisville was a nearly eight-hour trip there and back and I didn't have the energy to do it yet.

"Yes ma'am." Donna grinned. "We can make do with just these until you can get our new one in here."

"All right, then. I'll have the new one up to y'all soon as I can. Get ready though because I ain't haulin' that damn thing up this mountain by myself," I joked. "Was there anythin' else y'all needed?"

I watched as Donna and her guys looked at one another, their faces even more apprehensive than they'd been when they broke the news about the still to me.

"What's wrong?" I asked.

It was Donna who spoke up. "Miss Hannah, we know you married that Meza boy and we know we're supposed to be workin' with them from here on out but..." She paused, then trailed off and bit down hard on her bottom lip. "We just wanted to know if you were goin' to have them come up here with us too?"

Before I could answer, one of the guys spoke up, the gold cap on one of his front teeth glinting. "We don't mean to disrespect but we just ain't too sure about havin' them comin' in and gettin' a look at our process is all, ma'am."

"And it ain't just us." When Donna interjected, she had a little more confidence in her tone. "We know them down in the kitchen don't want them gettin' their hands on them mash recipes, either."

"Y'all don't have to worry about that," Clyde answered for me, his deep voice strong and sure.

"Right." I gave them a smile I hoped like hell was reassuring. "We're workin' with the Mezas on a few different fronts to make sure that what happened to Bobby Crenshaw don't happen to anybody else in either of our families. But this ain't one of those fronts. They'll keep away from our production and we do the same. Nobody is comin' in to step on your toes. You have my word on that."

I'd held a meeting with the leaders in every section of my organization after making my deal with Benicio. There had been plenty of grumbles about the partnership, but no outright objections. Luckily, it seemed that everyone understood this was a necessity; one that would be as short-lived as possible. I'd assumed everyone understood that the partnership, and my marriage with Javier, was only in place to make sure they were safe. Donna's words proved that confidence wasn't as warranted as I'd previously thought. Their concerns were valid, and they also made it clear I needed to make sure my people saw I was on their side above all else.

I hoped like hell what I was viewing as a personal sacrifice in my life wasn't going to look like I was prioritizing the Mezas over my family.

Clyde and I spent another hour or so with the stilling group before we made our way down to the kitchens. Luckily, they weren't in need of any expensive equipment so after we looked in on their base mash experiments, we were on our way back home.

When I got in, Javier was sitting in the living room with Cameron Kelly, one of my best runners and Sam, one of the many Meza cousins. The three of them were sipping at beers while sitting on my new couch, laughing together like they were old friends.

"Uh, hello," I said slowly, putting my purse down on the console next to the front door.

"Hey Hannah," Javier and Cameron answered me in tandem, twin smiles on their faces.

Sam greeted me with a quiet, respectful, "Hello."

I stood there silently with my eyebrows raised waiting for any of them to tell me what Cameron and Sam were doing in my house. None of them spoke up.

"Y'all need somethin'?" I tried to keep mine as light as possible.

Cameron cleared his throat and stood up from the couch, taking his baseball cap off of his head as he approached me. I hid my smile. The boy was twenty-three, exactly a decade younger than me, but the way he interacted with me sometimes made me feel like I was his actual elder. He gestured for Sam, who I believed was a year younger than him, to join him.

"We just wanted to come by and give you an update on that thing you put us on," Cameron said, his hazel eyes on mine.

I perked up immediately. Cam and Sam were only two of the few people we'd tasked with figuring out where the Ward family was stationed after they'd confronted us outside the clerk's office. Both Benicio and I had put people on it, and while we hoped they'd get back to us with answers quickly, I hadn't expected anything so soon.

"You found out where they're holed up?"

"We think they might have a couple'a places," Sam said. "But we talked to this dude whose daddy runs a landscaping company. Said he just signed a contract to do yard work for the Wards at some brand new, big ass mansion on some land outside Cumberland."

I snorted. It didn't seem like they gave a shit about being discreet. Maybe they didn't know people around our parts didn't take too well to a bunch of shitty rich folks moving in on their territory.

"Did y'all go by there?"

"Yes ma'am." Cam nodded. "Just this mornin'. Saw that white Porsche you described outside too."

"Fire ride," Sam said under his breath, earning himself a thump on the back of the head from his partner.

I held my breath, waiting for Sam to retaliate with a hit of his own or angry words, but he looked thoroughly admonished. It was almost ridiculous how happy I was to see the two of them somewhat getting along.

Javier seemed to appear out of thin air at my side. "Right outside Cumberland," he said quietly. "They're probably close to my family's place."

"Does Benicio know about this?" I asked all three of the men in front of me.

"No, ma'am," Sam answered. "He's still out of town so we came to you first to see what you wanted us to do. We figured Javier would pass the message along."

Javier snorted, but still agreed.

We thanked the men and sent them on their way, but not before telling them to stick close by that house. I wanted to know how many people came and went on a regular basis, whether or not they had their own shine making operation on the land. Hell, I wanted to know what they had for supper on Sunday nights. The more information we could get on those bastards the better.

After the guys left, Javier presented me with the other half of a huge hoagie he'd made for lunch. I was so tired that I performed one of my grandmother's cardinal sins—eating on the couch—while we caught up with each other.

"How'd it go today?" he asked, still sipping on his beer.

"It was all right." I shrugged, mouth stuffed full. "I've got to head to Louisville sometime soon to get a new still. One of ours is done for."

"It can't be fixed?"

"Wouldn't be worth the money spent."

Javier laid those brown eyes on me, his gaze intense underneath his slightly bushy brows. "Well, maybe you can make use of one of ours for the time bein'."

I pulled my eyes away from him, picking at some of the ingredients that had fallen from my sandwich. "I don't think that's such a good idea."

"I don't see why not," he pushed. "We're together now, right? It ain't like you're a stranger."

I thought back to the conversation I'd had with Donna and her guys earlier that morning. They'd been concerned about the Mezas getting too close. I'd been too, but my trip to Nashville with Javier had changed something in me. I was beginning to trust him and that was dangerous, especially when I didn't—couldn't—fully trust his father. I couldn't let my annoying attraction for him cloud my business. That would be dangerous in a shit ton of different ways.

"Sure." I tried to keep my tone light and conversational. "But I think we need to avoid gettin' unnecessarily tangled up, you know? It'll make things harder when this whole thing is over."

Javier stared at me. I was too much of a coward to look

back, but I could feel the heat coming off him even from across the room. I could only bear to turn my eyes to him when I heard him stand up out of his chair. His neck was bared as he drained the rest of his beer, a bit of the liquid dripping down into his shaggy beard as he gulped.

"Right," he drawled. "No tangles then."

I watched as he walked away from me, the muscles in his back and shoulders tight as he stiffly made his way up the stairs and to his room. By the time I heard him reach the top, I'd lost my appetite. And when his door closed, I felt a little sick to my stomach.

# CHAPTER 9

JAVIER

Lexington was the second-largest city in the state of Kentucky. Over three hundred thousand people lived there at any given time. I'd heard a lot of the locals say the city still managed to have a "small-town feel" despite its numbers, but it was never a statement that made any sense to me. Cumberland only had a little over two thousand people walking its streets in a good year. Hell, my graduating class in high school had barely fifty students in it. To me, Lexington had always felt like the biggest, most exciting, full place in the world even long after I'd learned differently.

Which meant it only made sense I'd run into my ex-wife in a grocery store near my abuelita's house.

My conversation with Hannah the day before had fucked my head up. After Nashville, I'd been positive she and I had been moving in the right direction. I wasn't claiming we were in love or anything, but I figured my wife had at least agreed to follow the terms we'd set and try to make our marriage work.

The second Hannah mentioned not wanting to get too "tangled" up with me, my mind immediately went back to that bed we'd shared. Our bodies had been tangled up together, pressing close, radiating heat. She hadn't seemed to have a big problem with it then, just like I hadn't.

I understood her concerns; our marriage had been built on a business deal. The rivalry between our families made that deal delicate. And, obviously, we had a lot on the line with our legacies, our histories, our lives. I got that Hannah needed to be cautious to keep the whole thing running smoothly but fuck, I didn't want her to have to be so cautious with me. I was trying my damnedest to be more open and honest than I'd ever been with anyone. Trying to do right by her, to be someone she could lean on, to be her damn husband. I was now starting to think that wasn't something Hannah was interested in from me.

I'd stormed off in a huff, a rude action I regretted but not enough to apologize for. The next morning, I left before I knew she'd be awake. The nearly three-hour drive from Harlan to Lexington helped me clear my head some, but the comforting arms of my grandmother gave me peace.

Abuelita had greeted me with smiles and kisses the same way she always did. I hadn't opened the floodgates to tell her what was wrong, but she'd sensed it anyway. Our brief greeting had been interrupted by her sending me off to the store to get ingredients to make my grandfather's *pozole*.

I was inside her favorite Mexican grocery store when I ran into Maritza.

I recognized her from her profile. She had her head down,

was feeling over some tomatillos. Her long, dark hair was up in a ponytail at the top of her head, and she was dressed casually in a pair of cut-off shorts and a tank top. She looked the same as she had the last time I'd seen her two years before. Only, this time, I wasn't looking shamefully at her distressed face as she packed the last of her belongings from our house into her brother's truck.

For a second, I considered turning around. The store was big enough that I could hide on the other side for a while. Like me, she had one of those handheld baskets instead of a big cart. Truthfully, I didn't want to see her. I didn't want to be confronted with my worst failure while I was currently staring down the barrel at another one that was surely coming my way soon.

Before I could make my decision, Maritza looked up and over, her light brown eyes landing directly on mine. She looked shocked for a second, eyes wide and lips slightly opened, but her expression changed just as quickly as it had appeared.

She put the tomatillos she was holding back on the crate and made her way over to me. I met her halfway until we were both standing in front of the plantains.

"Hey, Javier." Her voice was soft and husky, just like it had always been.

"Mari…" I trailed off with a smile.

It had been nearly two years since I'd last seen her and I didn't know what else to say.

"What are you doing here?" she asked.

I held up my basket, already filled with most of the things I needed. "Abuelita's making pozole for lunch."

Mari shook her head and laughed, some of her dark hair escaping her ponytail. "Just like mine. Eighty-something damn degrees and they're up making *caldo*."

I couldn't help but laugh along with her. My grandfather had always seemed to get the urge to make the dish when the outside temperatures were at their hottest.

She looked good, healthy, and happy with pink in her cheeks and laugh lines deep around her eyes. It was completely selfish of me to ask her anything about her life, but I needed to know.

"How have you been?"

I was almost surprised when Mari's face didn't crack and immediately become sad. Instead, she smiled, the crinkles on the sides of her eyes going deeper. It was shameful as hell of me, but I hadn't been expecting it. I wanted to slap *myself* in the face for having the audacity to assume I could still be the cause of any kind of pain for her.

"I've been good," she said. "Great, actually. My boyfriend and I just got back from Italy last night. We're having our first home-cooked meal in a few weeks. We're doing burgers."

"Did you have a good time in Italy?"

Mari had always wanted to go to Italy. It was something she'd talked about even before we'd gotten married. I'd promised to take her one day but never had.

"It was beautiful," she gushed. "Just like I knew it would be. And the food!" Her eyes rolled to the back of her head in a show of pleasure. "What about you, Javier? How have you been lately?"

"I've been good too. Workin' with Pop, some old, same old really. I uh—" I paused. "I got married a couple of weeks ago."

I wasn't ashamed or embarrassed to admit it. Those weren't emotions I could ever feel when it came to Hannah Hawkins and my relationship with her. But I still felt a bit of apprehension about telling Maritza. She knew better than anybody what a shitty partner I'd been. She'd experienced it firsthand. It wasn't her judgment I was scared of. My fear was tied to some of the last words she'd said to me. The ones telling me I'd probably always be incapable of being good to a woman because I had no idea how to really love one.

Mari didn't seem to know what to say. She stuttered for a couple of seconds, never taking her eyes off me.

"That...that's..." She searched for an adjective. "That's great, Javier. I'm happy for you. Truly."

Mari was obviously shocked but there was nothing about her words or her tone that sounded disingenuous. I wasn't surprised by that. I still maintained that my ex-wife was one of the most genuinely kind people I'd ever met. I was just glad our doomed relationship hadn't forced that trait out of her.

"Thank you, Mari." I smiled.

"Is it someone I know? Someone from Cumberland?"

Like my mother, Mari was a Lexington girl born and bred. Her parents had immigrated from Mexico before she was born. They'd found their home in Cardinal Valley, a neighbor-

JODIE SLAUGHTER

hood where Latino immigrants, like my mother's parents, had been fellowshipping for decades, and hadn't moved since. Mari loved her neighborhood and she'd given it up to come live with me in my neck of the woods, something I hadn't appreciated enough at the time. In the four years we were married, she made plenty of friends in Cumberland, but I doubted she knew Hannah personally.

"No, a woman from Harlan actually," I said. "Hannah Hawkins."

"Hawkins? Like...?"

I nodded with a chuckle. "Yeah, those Hawkins."

Mari knew about my family's business. She was an accountant who'd worked on our books as her day job for years. She hadn't been super clued in on all of our histories, but she obviously knew of our biggest rivals.

"I can't believe your dad was okay with that." She rolled her eyes.

"It was his idea actually." I paused, not necessarily wanting to tell her the grittier parts of my recent nuptials. "Said it would help make us stronger. He wasn't wrong."

Maritza gave her head a slow, exasperated shake. "You know, as hard as I try, I don't think I'll ever fully understand the way y'all do things up there."

"No." I laughed. "But you understand how important tradition is to keepin' a family strong."

For a second, Mari flashed me a look that made me think of the ones she used to give me during our first years together. When we were young and in love and before I was just her asshole husband who didn't know how to love her the right way. In those days, it had made me all weak-kneed and starry-eyed but now, it just made me feel a distant fondness.

"You're right," she said. "That's one thing we'll always be on the same page about."

I couldn't help the words that poured from me, words that I should have said years before. "Mari, look, I know it's been a while and we've both moved on but I..." I rubbed a hand on the back of my neck when the flesh heated. "I'm sorry. Truly. I should have been better for you."

"Yes, you should have." She walked up to me and lay a hand on my shoulder. "But I've forgiven you, Javier. We were so young and neither of us was mature enough emotionally to have as big a responsibility as being married."

"You were always way more emotionally mature than I was."

"I was." She laughed. "But the Javier from six years ago never would have had it in him to admit he was wrong."

Shame flooded through me again. She was right. The Javier she'd known would have outright refused to have such a difficult conversation. He would have cowered...just like I had with Hannah.

Shit.

Maybe I wasn't so different after all. In that second, I felt like a child again. I felt like that cowardly little man who had entered a marriage before he had any of the tools to sustain it. How many times had I walked away from Maritza during a disagreement? How many times had I holed myself up in our kitchens or in my grandparents' house instead of facing my wife? Too goddamn many.

Hannah had pissed me off. She'd disregarded me and it made me mad enough to spit and just as disappointed. My head started filling with all the things I should have said to her, with everything I should have expressed instead of holding it in like some repressed asshole.

I'd entered my marriage with Hannah determined not to make the same mistakes I had with Mari. To keep myself from being a disappointment to yet another wife. How the fuck did I expect to do that if I kept doing the same dumb shit?

"Mari." I looked down at her. "It was good seeing you, but I have to go. I have something I have to do."

She stepped back with a smile. "Okay, Javier. It was good seeing you too. You look good."

I leaned down and laid a kiss on her forehead.

"Hey," I called to her as I backed away. "Stop by and see Abuelita sometime, huh? She says she misses playing dominoes with you."

"I'll go see her." She laughed. "You be good to that new wife of yours, Javier. Be better this time around."

I couldn't do shit but grin at her.

That was exactly what I was going to do.

# CHAPTER 10

HANNAH

"I don't appreciate you dismissin' me."

I nearly dropped the phone in my hand when Javier crashed into the living room with a big paper bag full of groceries and a voice full of conviction. He'd been gone by the time I woke up with not so much as a text telling me where he was going or when he'd be back. I'd spent the day trying to push down my annoyance. It was completely hypocritical of me. It wasn't like I hadn't spent time avoiding him in the couple weeks we'd been married.

"Excuse me?" I asked, laying my phone on the couch next to me.

"Yesterday, you dismissed me durin' our conversation. You said some shit that didn't make no damn sense and completely dismissed me in the process." Javier's eyes weren't hardened, but they had the same determined glint I heard in his voice.

"I'm not sure how what I said didn't make any sense," I shot back.

I knew exactly what I'd said to him, word for damn word. I'd spent my entire ride home from Black Mountain rehearsing it in my head.

The face Javier made at me would have made me laugh if it didn't have me close to squirming. He looked done, completely unimpressed with my explanation. He came closer, sitting in the chair on the other side of the coffee table in front of me. It was the same position we'd been in during our little talk the day before.

"You said it was best we didn't get too tangled up with each other." He leaned forward as he spoke, his forearms resting on his strong thighs. "What the hell is that supposed to mean?"

"Exactly what it sounds like." I shrugged. "I just want to keep things from bein' messier than they're already goin' to be when we separate. We already agreed to keep certain parts of our business out of this."

Javier sighed and ran a hand down his face. The red undertones in his light brown skin became a little more pronounced. I could tell he was trying not to let his frustration show.

"Sure we did," he conceded. "And I'm fine with keepin' that part of our lives separate, but that ain't all you meant and you know it, Hannah."

I scoffed even though I knew he was right.

Javier continued. "When we were discussin' the terms of this arrangement, you agreed that you would actually try to make this work. How are we supposed to do that when you can't stop focusin' on what's goin' to happen in the end?"

I clenched my eyes shut. I couldn't look at him anymore. I hadn't expected much going into our marriage. I'd expected Javier to treat me with the respect I deserved. I'd also expected him to mostly stay out of my way, to pretty much be a stranger until we parted ways.

Out of all the things I'd assumed Javier would be, I hadn't thought he'd be nearly as consuming as he was. I felt his presence all over my house. His scent lingered in our shared hallway, the kitchen, hell, on my couch cushions even. When I was out without him, I was constantly catching myself thinking about him, even things as simple as what he was doing or what color shirt he'd chosen to wear. Javier didn't give me butterflies, he made hummingbirds sing and flutter on the inside of every part of me.

I was a pro at infatuation, the beginning stage of relationships when everything was sweet and smiley. I was a great flirt and enjoyed having fun. I'd even been in love a couple of times, but I'd still managed to maintain a certain amount of distance. With Javier, that was starting to feel more impossible every day. Not to mention the doubts that lingered about the way my connection with the Mezas made me look to my people. I was trying to protect myself on two fronts, and I was honestly floored as to why Javier didn't seem to be doing the same thing.

"How could I not focus on that, Javier? This thing has an expiration date whether we get rid of the Wards or not. I hope like hell that we do, but when that happens, you're not goin' to be here with me to make sure I can be strong enough to keep my family standin'."

"Who says?" he asked.

"What?"

Javier ran a tongue over his full lips, and I followed the motion until the plump flesh gleamed in the sunlight that filtered in through the thin white curtains in the room.

"Who says I'm not goin' to be here when this shit with the Wards is done?"

"Oh please." I rolled my eyes to keep them from bulging.

"I'm serious, Hannah. You think I'm sittin' here all eager to get divorced again?"

I didn't say anything, but I stared him down, searching for something in his eyes or expression. Something that would show me even the smallest amount disingenuousness that I could grab onto. I didn't find anything, and the knowledge he actually meant what he said was enough to make my stomach start doing flips again.

"Javier," I had no choice but to breathe out his name, "that's a ridiculous thing to say."

"Is it?" he asked. "I don't think it's ridiculous at all that I don't want to have another marriage fail by my hand."

"I can understand that, but you know this is different. This marriage won't be failin'. There's nothin' to fail. It ain't real."

My voice sounded desperate as hell and I didn't even have the nerve to be embarrassed by it now.

"What if it could be?" Javier stared me down, those deep brown eyes intense and unyielding.

I wasn't ready to fully acknowledge what he was suggesting so I played up my ignorance. "What if it could be what?"

"Real, Hannah." The way he said my name made me shiver. "Our marriage could be real. It could grow into somethin' real and good. We could both be happy."

"So, in our negotiations, when you said you wanted to 'try' you meant…"

Javier shrugged. "I meant that I wanted us to try not to be assholes to each other but I guess…" He paused. "Yeah, that's what I meant. I want to see if we can turn this into somethin' that ain't doomed. Somethin' we can both be proud of."

The thought made my throat tighten up a bit. What he was suggesting was ridiculous but it also set me on fire.

"We can't court each other, Javier. We're already married." A part of me was willing to try every excuse possible to deny how into the idea I was.

"Sure we can, and if it doesn't work out, our breakup will just involve a little more paperwork than normal."

I snorted. "Where do we even start? We already live together."

"Well." My husband stood up and held a hand out to me. I took it, his large palms warm and dry, but touching him wasn't even close to being unpleasant. "You can start by makin' good on your promise from our negotiations and cookin' dinner with me tonight."

"I can do that." I nodded. "What are we having?"

Javier ran a hand along the back of his neck the way he sometimes did when he was feeling embarrassed or uncertain. I had no idea why he would have been feeling that way at the moment, especially not after his bold ass convinced me to start dating him two weeks after we'd gotten married.

"Pozole," he said. "You ever had it?"

I shook my head. I'd never even heard of it.

His grin was almost wolfish as he led me to the kitchen by my hand. "You've been missin' out, wife."

A little while later, Javier and I were staring over a pot of simmering water and pork shoulder, breathing in the scent of seasoned meat. Closing the lid, he disappeared behind me for a moment before he came back with my old wooden chopping board, a knife, and a couple cloves of garlic. I moved my knife with absolutely no grace while I watched him expertly cut up an onion. He reminded me of one of the celebrity chefs I watched on TV all the time.

"You're good at that." It was the first real thing I'd said to him since our conversation in the living room.

Javier flashed me a bright, toothy smile. I bit down on my bottom lip.

"Thank you."

"You learned that from your granddaddy?"

I remembered him saying he'd worked in the man's restaurant as a kid. I'd assumed Javier had worked as a busboy or dishwasher, but it was obvious he'd learned a bit more than the right way to use a commercial sink sprayer.

"Yep." He nodded. "I first got in the kitchen with him when I was about five and didn't leave until he passed last year."

Something in Javier's face told me he didn't want any condolences, so I didn't give him any.

"Did you want to be a chef?" I asked.

He shook his head as he finished chopping his onion,

moving to pile it next to the garlic I'd cut. "No, I just like food, and I liked bein' around him."

That made sense. I nodded, watching as he added the onion, garlic, and some bay leaves to the boiling water.

"We'll wait to make the soup until the pork is cooked a little more," Javier murmured before he sat down at the little kitchen table and looked up at me. "What about you? You like to cook?"

"Not really." I chuckled. "Mama always said it was important to know how to take care of yourself, but I don't really like it. I make a mean ass bowl of cereal though."

The smile on Javier's face was so soft it made my knees a little weak. I had to sit down.

"Tell me somethin' about her," he requested softly.

"Who, my mother?"

He nodded. "I know of her generally, obviously, but you talk so much about her and I want to know more. Somethin' interestin'."

I thought about his request for a few moments. Mama had been the most complex person I'd ever met. Layers and layers and layers of shit I hadn't had nearly enough time to peel back before she was gone. Joy Hawkins had been funny, demanding, kind, mean, smart, and cunning. She was everything, and I was sure I had at least a hundred stories for each of those traits.

"One time, when me and Nicole were in elementary school, there was this kid who kept fuckin' with us. He used to throw shit at us when we walked home, get other kids to be mean to us, call us all kinds of slurs and shit, you know how it is." Javier nodded emphatically. I continued. "So, our teacher wouldn't do shit about it. She never told him to stop, didn't send anything home to his parents, nothin'. After a couple months, Mama got tired of us comin' home cryin' so she went down to the school. Instead of goin' to my teacher, she barged into the principal's office and had us sit there while she threatened to have almost every teacher in the school arrested and fired for possessin' moonshine and having alcohol in a dry county. By the time she finished, that woman was damn near in tears and when we went to school the next day, our teacher had all but rolled out the red carpet for us. Our little school district always made sure nobody fucked with the Hawkins kids after that."

By the time I was finished with my story, Javier looked incredibly impressed.

"Damn."

"Mama was always my biggest champion." I smiled. "She was merciful about a lot of shit, but never when it came to people messin' with her babies."

"What about your dad? You lost him when you were little, right?"

It was hard to keep things a secret in towns as small as the ones we lived in. Everyone knew everything about everybody, and I'd always found it amazing no one ever seemed to know the true story about why my father wasn't around. It wasn't one I enjoyed sharing, outside of my immediate family. Lex was the only person I'd ever talked about him with and even then, it was only because she was part of the story.

I didn't know what the hell came over me but whatever it

was sent that story tumbling from my lips easier than it ever had.

"Nah, he's still alive." I rolled my eyes. "Lives with his second wife and their son in Bowling Green. He never really liked it here and he and Mama had some issues. She had an affair and he left her, which is fine, but he left us too."

I left out the parts about the man Mama had an affair with being Alexis' dad, the promises to visit that never turned into anything, and about the fact that he could never even be bothered to send cards on our birthdays. It all seemed so dark and heavy and that wasn't what I wanted at the moment. I wanted to sit at the kitchen table with Javier, forget about everything weighing down on my shoulders, and enjoy the soup he claimed somehow tasted better when it was hot outside.

He seemed to sense that I didn't want to speak on the subject anymore without me having to voice that. When leaned back in his chair with those long legs spread out a bit in front of him with a lazy smile on his face, I sighed with relief.

"Well." He drawled out the word. "Miss Joy seems to have done a good job all on her own."

"Corny," I coughed.

Javier pointed one of his fingers at me in a fake reprimand. "Hey! What did I tell you before? I ain't corny, I'm honest!"

The only answer he was met with from me was a mocking laugh.

For the next hour or so, Javier and I sat at the table across from each other. We didn't bring up the fact that we were apparently "dating" each other, but the energy was absolutely different. The conversation was relatively light, but I learned a lot about him. I found out he was nineteen when he lost his virginity, that he'd somehow managed to never break a bone, and even that he'd briefly tried to learn how to ride a motorcycle but gave up when he realized he hated falling.

By the time the pork was fully cooked, I felt like I had a better grasp on who Javier Meza was as a person. He was quiet and funny, always down for a laugh and a good time. But he also had things in his past that had obviously clouded how he saw himself. I figured that had something to do with his first marriage. As curious as I was to hear more about that, I didn't push him to talk about it. If he and I were supposed to be getting to know each other, I figured it would all come to light at some point.

Javier did the majority of the work when it came to preparing the rest of the pozole. I did a little more prep work —some chopping and seasoning here and there—but he was a beast in the kitchen. It wasn't a quick dish to make. Things had to simmer and cook for what felt like forever before he was finally spooning the fragrant, dark red soup into bowls for us to eat.

He watched me as I took my first bite. The taste hit me immediately. It was hot and warm and so full of flavor I had to take a second bite immediately.

"Jesus, this is good," I groaned. I enjoyed Mexican food, but we didn't have any restaurants in Harlan. The closest thing was some shitty chain joint near Cumberland, and what they sold was the furthest thing imaginable from what Javier had placed in front of me.

"I'm glad you like it." His full lips quirked in a small smile.

"It's the best thing I've eaten in a good minute." The compliments wouldn't stop flowing. "You really put your foot in this one."

We cleared our bowls in what felt like no time. I even sat at the kitchen table, waiting patiently as Javier finished off his second helping. He'd done most of the cooking, but he still insisted on helping me clean up afterward.

"What made you decide to make this?" I asked, handing him a dish to dry off.

That sheepish look appeared on his face again. "I didn't, not really. I went to see my grandmother this morning because I was feelin' off after our conversation yesterday, and she was goin' to make it to help me feel better like my grandfather did when I was little."

My hand was still wet and a little sudsy from the dish-water when I lay it on his bare arm right under the edge of his black t-shirt. "I'm sorry, for what I said, Javier." I hoped like hell my voice sounded as sincere as I felt. "I don't think I said that earlier but I really am. I don't want to make you feel dismissed again so I'm goin' to try to be less of an asshole. Like, consciously and whatnot."

"Thank you, Hannah." His tone was soft. "I appreciate that."

"Anyway, continue."

"Right. Well, she sent me out to the store to get the stuff to make it and," he took a pause but I didn't know why, "I ran into Maritza, my ex-wife."

I stopped my washing as a foreign feeling welled up in me. I couldn't put a name on it, but I was sure it wasn't jealousy. It almost felt like fear. Fear the next words out of Javier's mouth would be him realizing he was still in love with his ex or something. He made sure to keep his eyes on my face as he spoke.

"She looked great and was doin' well too, but seein' her made me realize I shouldn't have run away from the fact that I needed to confront you about how you made me feel. I needed to stop doin' the same little boy shit I did when I was with her and act like I was grown. So, I just left out of there with all the shit I'd picked up and brought it home to you. I called my Abuelita on the way to let her know what was up."

"So, you just cooked me dinner with ingredients you were supposed to take to your granny?"

My mind was racing with the speed of all the information he'd just given me. Javier running into his ex, rushing home to call me out on my bullshit, and leaving his grandmother high and dry, it was all so much. Every part of it left me feeling a different kind of way. I was nervous, giddy, flattered, and a bunch of other things I couldn't name all at once.

The grin he gave me added another unmentionable emotion to the fold. "She'll be all right," he joked. "She said she expects me to make her a pot when she comes up here to meet you."

His voice went from playful to serious in the span of a single sentence. I rinsed the last dish, not saying a word as I handed the skillet to him and dried my hands off with a clean cloth hanging from the cabinet under the sink. I waited until my throat felt less restricted to look at him again.

"You want me to meet your grandmother?" I asked.

"She likes to meet all my wives." He chuckled.

"Javier…" I reached out to him, gripping his bicep.

"Yes, Hannah. I want you to meet my grandmother."

I found myself unconsciously stepping closer to him. I moved until our bodies were touching. We weren't pressed together tightly, not like we had been in our hotel room in Nashville or in the speakeasy, but much closer than we'd been since we'd come home.

"That's big, Javier."

I knew how close Javier was with his mother's parents. How, even after his grandfather had passed, he made sure to maintain a strong relationship with his granny.

"It doesn't have to be today or even next week, but she's important to me and you…you're my wife. It means a lot to me that you meet her."

The thought made me nervous as all hell. I'd never really met a man's family before and that was with normal, non-arranged relationships. A faint, niggling voice in the back of my head told me to deny him. It told me that our relationship was too young and too shaky to do things like that. I had no choice but to ignore it. I thought back to the conversation we'd had earlier, to the promise I'd made to consider his feelings and put some actual effort into our relationship. If Javier said it was important to him, I'd do it, even if it scared the hell out of me.

"Okay," I replied simply, afraid that if I talked any more my nervousness would show.

Somehow, Javier found a way to get even closer to me. His strong arms wrapped around my waist, hands splaying out in the middle of my back. I could feel my nipples harden the second my breasts were pushed further on his chest.

"Thank you, Hannah." His voice was a little more gravelly than it had been before.

His warm breath fanned across my face. It still smelled a little like the pozole we'd eaten, but I didn't find it unpleasant at all.

"You're welcome, Javier."

I had no idea what we were doing, why we were standing so close, why Javier was looking down at me like he wanted to swallow me whole, and why I was positive my face looked the same way to him.

"Hannah..." He sighed out my name and I felt my body hum. Something tinged in my lower belly.

His gaze made me feel weightless, and I relaxed in his arms, almost like my body was preparing itself for what I felt was about to happen.

"Yes?" I would have been embarrassed at how breathy my voice as if I hadn't been so caught up in him.

"Would you like for me to kiss you?"

I nodded.

I felt his thumbs stroke my back through my thin t-shirt as his dark eyes became a little more hooded. His tongue ran over his lips, and he leaned in towards me until our noses and foreheads were touching.

"I'm goin' to now," he said.

I got there first, though, moaning softly as soon as my lips touched his. Javier's kisses matched his personality exactly, warm and confident and ridiculously sexy. The first brush of his tongue made me shiver and clutch at him. I had to fight the urge to grind against him like I was in heat.

He and I spent what felt like an eternity making out like teenagers against my kitchen sink, yielding to each other, constantly chasing the pleasure we'd found. By the time we pulled away, we were breathing heavy, our chests heaving with the intensity of our actions.

His mouth was red and swollen. I leaned up again to peck him once, then twice. Javier smiled at me, his teeth dragging my bottom lip out just a little before I felt his tongue there again.

My brain was racing, blood rushing to my ears, and the only thing I could hear was Javier's pounding heart when I rested my ear on his chest. The arms around me tightened, and I shuddered at the rumbling feeling when he finally spoke again.

"I'm goin' to make you so happy, wife." His voice sounded wrecked. "Just wait and see."

# CHAPTER 11

JAVIER

Three days later, the loud ringing of my cell phone woke me up before five in the morning. I groaned as I rolled over, the tense muscles in my back stretching as I peeked out the window to see the sky was still black.

"What?" I answered, not bothering to check the caller ID.

"Javier!"

I sat up, immediately recognizing my cousin Marc's frantic voice. "Yeah? What's wrong?"

"Somethin's gone down." I could hear the chaos in the background, people shouting and things falling. "Somebody set our kitchen on fire."

"What?" I ground out, my voice sounding more panicked than I meant it to be.

Marc's breathing became more labored by the second. "Yeah, we were sleepin' down the hill and woke up when we started smellin' the smoke. It's still burnin' right now."

It was hard for me to wrap my head around what he was

saying. I could hardly think; my own lungs felt like they were filling with smoke even miles away from the fire.

"Were y'all makin' anything?" We didn't keep our stock in the kitchens, but if there had been any significant amount of alcohol in the building when it caught fire, I could only imagine how bad things would get.

"No." Marc swallowed. "We were cleanin' out the stills when it happened. Wasn't no shine in there."

"Was anybody hurt?" That was the most important thing at the moment.

"No. Jerry twisted his ankle runnin' down the hill, but that's it."

"Good, good." I was up and out of the bed, my phone held between my shoulder and my ear as I searched the dark room for some clothes. "What about the fire? It ain't spreadin' is it?"

"The guys used the emergency hose to get it down." He sounded distraught. "It's containin' itself, but it's takin' everything with it."

I swallowed hard. We'd put a lot of time, work, and money into that kitchen. To think that somebody had come in and destroyed it in a matter of minutes made me want to hurt something.

"All right." I pulled my jeans up. "Hold tight, stay safe. I'll be up there as soon as I can."

"Okay, boss."

"Marc, listen, if that fire starts spreadin', ya'll get the hell out of there. I don't care what you have to leave behind."

"Sure," he said softly and then hung up the phone. Marc

had agreed, but I wasn't convinced he'd actually follow my orders. That only made me move faster.

I was dialing Pop's number seconds later, listening as the phone rang five times before he answered.

"Boy, do you know what time it is?"

They'd gotten back from Louisville in the late evening, so I knew how tired he and Mami must have been. I would have felt guilty if I'd been calling for any reason other than the shitshow that had found its way to our doorstep.

I cut to the chase, rushing out an explanation of what had happened. My father's fury was completely uncontained. By the time we got off the phone, I was almost positive he was about to commit a murder.

I'd left my room and was seconds from flying down the stairs when I passed Hannah's. Her lights were off and while I knew she was in there, I also knew there was no way she was awake. I considered just leaving, going to handle my family's business and telling her about what had happened later. Both because I didn't want to disturb her sleep and because I was unsure about how she would react. We'd agreed to keep business matters out of our relationship, one that had only started three days ago. But this was more than discussing distribution routes or still donations. This was my family's life being burned to the ground. We were already working together and, beyond that, we were a community, rivals or not.

I knocked first, making sure my knuckles rapped on the door loud enough to wake her out of her sleep, and then opened it. She sat up, lines from her pillow on her face and her scarf wrapped around her head. Much like my Pop, I didn't give her a chance to be mad at me before I explained the situation. Nor did I get the chance to appreciate her thick thighs and soft stomach as she slid out of bed and into some clothes after she insisted on joining me.

The drive to our kitchen in Cumberland from Harlan normally took about thirty minutes, but I made it in a little over fifteen. Hannah was on the phone the entire ride, calling her people and requesting we get all hands on deck to deal with the issue.

I didn't know what the Hawkins stilling setup was like, but I knew they kept their spot hidden away in the mountains somewhere. The Mezas didn't. We kept our kitchen and stilling site together in a huge souped up barn on a big plot of farmland. For years, we'd insisted this made everything easier for us. We didn't feel the need to hide our operation under a brush of dark fir trees. Everyone knew who we were, from the locals to the county deputies. Everybody who couldn't be paid off with discounted liquor was paid off with cash, and it had been that way for longer than I'd been alive. The most trouble we'd had was idiot teenagers trying to break in, in the middle of the night, to steal our supply.

When I saw smoke billowing from a pile of black rubble as we pulled up to the farm, I couldn't help but think of the countless things we could have done differently to make it harder for the Wards to get their hands on us.

The scene was surprisingly calm. I could still hear the rubble being engulfed by the dampening flames, but that was about it. My guys were all huddled together around their trucks with their eyes wide.

"Jesus Christ." I looked over to see my parents standing next to my SUV. I got out, resisting the urge to run into my mother's arms the way I would have as a child.

"It's all gone," I said to my father. "Everything."

"No, it isn't," Mami ground out. "We've got a couple backup stills we can set up in the barn at home."

Stills weren't cheap. We may not have had ones as big as the ones commercial companies used, but they were a hell of a lot bigger than the steel barrels and plastic we'd started out with. Mama was right. We had old ones on hand for emergencies, but they were only used as backups for a reason. They were smaller and raggedy and didn't produce wares that were up to our standard. Replacing the six stills we had would be nearly thirty grand. It was doable; we had money in the bank for situations like these, but it was another thing to build the kitchen from the ground up again.

"That ain't enough to go on as normal," Pop said. "We'd be losin' a hell of a lot of money and buyers the longer we go."

"That's better than nothing, Benny," she said softly, her hand on his arm.

I turned to my own wife and looked on as she watched the smoke billow up into the sky. I wondered what she was thinking. Our downfall might mean better business for the Hawkins, but I had a hard time imagining her being happy about it. Hannah must have felt my eyes on her because she looked up too, and when our eyes locked, I could see the remorse in hers.

She came closer to us, her arms crossed over her chest as

she opened and closed her mouth a couple of times like she was trying to figure out what to say.

What was there to say during a time like this?

Suddenly, her shoulders squared a bit, and her jaw tightened. "You'll use ours," she said, leaving no room for arguments. We found a way though.

"What?" my mother exclaimed.

My father didn't say a word as he stared at her, his bushy brows drawn.

"I thought we just had this conversation a few days ago," I said quietly. "In fact, if I remember it the right way, it was a fight. Didn't we agree not to do this kind of business together?"

"This is different, Javier."

"And how is that?" Pop took the words right out of my mouth.

"This ain't somethin' of your own doin'," she said. "This is them." Hannah pointed outward at nothing. "And we agreed not to let them beat us, right? Well, if y'all don't get on your feet with a quickness, we're all done."

I wanted to pull her to the side and talk about it some more, ask her if she was sure about the decision she was making to make sure it wasn't going to change our tentative agreement too much. But, I didn't. We didn't have the time to sit and wait and talk about our feelings. I also didn't want to plant any seeds of doubt in her head. We needed Hannah, and we needed her family and their resources, as hard as it was to admit.

"How would this work? I can't imagine your people would be too kind to us all in their faces every day."

Hannah shrugged. Her arms were now at her sides, her small hands clenched into fists. "You'll just have to do it at night like they use to way back when. I'll make sure my people clear out by eight, and y'all make sure you do the same by eight the next mornin'."

"Your people don't work through the night?" Mami questioned. "This won't get in the way of your own production?"

"Oh, it will." Hannah chuckled, but it wasn't a happy one. "And they're goin' to be mad as hell about it, but I'm in charge for a reason and I make the decisions. We can handle the new hours for now, so long as this is temporary."

"It will be." My father pushed past me to stand in front of Hannah. "We'll make sure we get ourselves up and runnin' as soon as possible."

"That's all I ask." Hannah bowed her head a little.

My father held a hand out for her to shake. The gesture was long and lasted for a little longer than it should have. I knew they both had a million thoughts and emotions running through their heads. It was probably one of the first times they'd felt something positive about each other.

Mami pushed past me too, but instead of a handshake, she drew Hannah in for a hug, my wife reluctantly wrapping her arms around her. My mother whispered something in her ear I didn't catch, but when I saw Hannah's arms tighten in response, I knew it must have been more than a simple thank you.

I was next, unable to stop myself from raising a hand to her full cheek to stroke as Mami joined Pop again.

"You have no idea…" I stopped, completely at a loss for words.

"Shhh." Her thumb touched my lips. "We can talk about it later. I know you're probably dyin' to express your feelins and shit."

She was right, I was. I wanted to express my gratefulness to her in any way I could. Now, I settled for pursing my lips, giving her warm thumb a kiss.

I pulled away when we heard sirens in the distance. I had no idea who'd called the fire department, but the closest fire department was nearly an hour away from the farm—so was the closest sheriff's station.

They came speeding up the dirt path, two cop cars and a fire engine so bright it lit up the dark sky.

"Now we have to deal with this bullshit," Pop mumbled, straightening out the T-shit he wore before turning to me. "Y'all go on and get some sleep. We'll handle the rest of this. Just meet us at the house in a couple of hours."

"A few hours," Mami corrected. "If I don't get back to sleep soon, I'll be the one setting some fires."

———

There was nothing about my childhood home that would have clued somebody in on the fact the family that lived there ran one of the largest moonshine making operations in Appalachia. It was neither a sprawling mansion or a one-room shack. Compared to some of the other houses in Cumberland, it was relatively new. Pop had bought it when it was only a few years old from some family after Mami realized she was pregnant with me in eighty-three. With four bedrooms, a finished basement, and a formal dining room we never used, the Mezas were luckier than most but still humble.

It was a traditional looking house, with a long front porch, an off-white coloring, and a front door Mami loved to have repainted a different color whenever she felt the spirit. It was powder blue when Hannah and I showed up to see my parents at a quarter 'til noon. The plan had been to go home and sleep for a little while before the meeting, but I'd been too wired to do anything but pace. At one point, I'd given up trying to be still and cleaned the kitchen, cut the grass, and did two loads of laundry.

By the time Hannah and me needed to leave, I was damn near ready to cry with relief over the fact that we were finally about to come to some kind of solution, and even more fuming than I'd been while watching our kitchen burn.

I let us into the house with my spare key and noticed two suitcases sitting on the hardwood floor next to the front door. We headed towards the voices coming from the kitchen, and they stopped as soon as we entered.

"My Javi," Mami cooed as she came over to wrap me up in a tight hug.

"Hey, Ma."

My father and Hannah greeted each other a little less stiffly than they had before.

"No Clyde today?" Pop asked Hannah as my mother approached her with arms wide.

"No, he had some family things to take care of. It's just me today."

I'd been with Hannah this morning when Clyde called and revealed that one of his aunts in Louisville was in the hospital, so he'd be out of town for a few days. I couldn't help but notice the face she'd made when she mentioned she was the only person on her side who would be in our meeting today. I wanted to correct her, tell her we were supposed to be a unit, but I didn't. Our agreement to try a relationship only went so far. I had no intentions of ever fucking her over, nor did I think my parents did either, but I was a Meza in everything, including the name. Now that we'd been attacked so thoroughly, my loyalty to my family was stronger than it had ever been. But that didn't mean I was going to leave her out in the cold.

Hannah and I sat across the kitchen island from my parents. The positioning didn't go unnoticed, especially not by my father who looked over us with his eyes slightly narrowed. As dedicated as I was to my family, I wanted to present a united front with my wife, so I didn't acknowledge his look as I laid an arm along the back of Hannah's chair.

"What are we thinkin'?" My father threw the question out.

"I'm thinkin' we need to hit them as hard as they hit us and put some fear in them while we're at it," I replied darkly.

"Javier's right," Hannah agreed. "We might not have realized it before, but the time for playin' offense is over."

"Well, we know where they live now right?" Mami asked. "We already have people watching them. It shouldn't be hard to prove to them that they're far from untouchable when we know how to get our hands on them."

Mami sat forward in her seat a bit, her eyes lit up with the possibilities of her own suggestion. All of five-foot-four with a soft voice and a pleasant smile to match, a lot of people made the mistake of assuming Alma Meza was a wholesome southern belle. For the most part, she was, amazing enough to give someone the shirt off her back. Her kindness knew no bounds. But the second she felt like someone had threatened her or her family, she pulled no punches. I was beginning to see it was a trait she and Hannah had in common.

"You thinkin' we set a fire of our own?" I asked her.

"No," my father said. "It needs to be a little more extreme than that."

Hannah sucked in a breath. The suggestion sounded ominous—and it was—but I knew Pop. He wouldn't take it that far if he could help it, and we still had a few options on the table. Hoping to comfort her, one of my thumbs found a spot of skin on her side her tank top wasn't covering and stroked the soft flesh there.

"Them rich bastards don't give a fuck about losing that mansion to a fire," he continued. "Give them a couple of days and they'll have already found a new one."

We all sat silently for a few moments, our thoughts whirring as we tried to come up with a solution.

"Do you remember when your daddy tried to have my

mama kidnapped after my granddaddy tried to steal some of his distribution routes?" Hannah asked, looking at my father.

Pop wasn't the type of man to ever look sheepish, but his brown cheeks flushed just a bit. "I remember Joy pullin' a shotgun on the two guys my daddy put on the job."

"Well, what do you want to bet none of the people in that house are as good a shot as Mama was?"

"Shit." Mami sat back in her chair with an impressed look on her face.

"It can't be some low-level goon though," I said. "We need to go right for the throat."

"The sons then." Hannah smirked. "Carver and Avery."

Pop nodded. "That way we can show our strength and bring the old man out of his hidin' place at the same time."

"When do you want to do this then?" I looked around at everyone in the room.

It was my mother who answered. "The sooner the better. If they think we're still scramblin' to fix the mess they made, they won't see us comin'."

We spent the next two hours discussing the matter at hand. We figured out who would do the actual kidnapping, where we would keep the Wards, and what lengths we absolutely wouldn't stoop to once we got them.

They had less than twenty-four hours of freedom before we took it away from them, the same way they'd taken my family's life work.

I couldn't keep the small smile off my face as I drove Hannah and me home. She was staring at me with an amused look when I pulled into the dirt driveway next to the house.

We both got out of the car, but instead of heading on in the house, Hannah came around front, smiling up at me as we stood with our thighs touching the warm grill.

"What?" I asked.

"Nothin', you're just...you're cute is all."

"You ain't lyin' there, but I'm happy too. Seems like we're finally goin' to bring these motherfuckers down."

"I think so too." She sighed. "I'm so ready for this shit to be over." Hannah stopped, her eyes widening a bit. "Not this." She waved a finger between us. "Just this in general."

"I know what you meant." I chuckled, stepping closer to her. "Me too. When we're done with this mess, we can focus on this." I mimicked her with my own finger.

"I..." She swallowed. "I don't think I'd hate that."

"That's a hell of an encouragement, wife."

Hannah smiled wide and leaned up a bit until her full, soft lips were brushing up against mine. "You know how much I aim to please my little husband."

# CHAPTER 12

HANNAH

I couldn't help the high-pitched noise that left me when Javier growled playfully and grabbed me up by my waist before he kissed me. It had only been a few days since we'd kissed for the first time, but his mouth on mine was already starting to feel familiar. That didn't make it boring, though. I still shivered when his tongue touched mine, and my body still melted into his the tighter he held me.

Javier pulled away too soon for my liking, drawing a whine from the back of my throat. "Remember earlier, at the farm, when I told you you had no idea what it meant to me that you're lettin' us use your kitchens?" he asked.

"Javier, what? Fuck all that. I just want you to keep kissin' me."

"That's exactly what I'm tryin' to make happen, wife. I want to thank you, show you how grateful I am you did somethin' so nice for my family."

"With kisses?" I asked with an eyebrow raised.

Javier nodded.

"Well good." I pressed my body up against him and tilted my face up. "Kiss away."

He shook his head, and I could see his dark eyes glinting. I narrowed my own.

"I want to give you my gratitude someplace other than that pretty mouth of yours."

My heart sped up when I realized what it meant. It wasn't a hot day at all, and the sun was planted firmly behind a thick covering of clouds with the faint scent of rain in the air, but I still started to feel hot behind the collar.

"Jesus."

"Only if you're interested in that." I could see the sincerity in his face. "If not, I'll just cook you another pot of pozole or change the oil in your car to show my thanks instead."

I thought about it. Everything in my body screamed yes. My nipples had gone hard at the mere suggestion, and I could feel my pussy swelling between my thighs. The thought of Javier's handsome face peeking up at me, covered in my wetness, made my belly thrum. But I wondered if doing something sexual with Javier so soon would prematurely ruin the relationship we were trying to build.

I snorted out loud at the thought. My last semi-serious relationship had started after a post-club hookup and lasted nearly two years. Sure, I was years removed from that man and it hadn't worked out anyway, but the point still stood. All those rules about when it was "acceptable" to sleep with someone you were dating were bullshit. Either Javier and I would work out or we wouldn't, but I refused to let myself believe we were doomed to fail because I let him go down on me a few days into the relationship.

"I can change my own oil." I flexed one of the hands I had on his hips. "And as good as your pozole was, I think I'd rather you show me your gratitude the way you were originally thinkin'."

Javier didn't need any further convincing. In a second, he had me propped up with my legs around his waist. I felt as giddy as I had when he picked me up at Liza's speakeasy the first time. I hadn't been picked up at all since I was a little girl, let alone with so much ease. It was a feeling that always made my belly do flip flops.

Our groins brushed and I could feel how hard he was through the thick denim of his jeans.

"Uh-uh," I said when he began to walk the path towards the house. "I want it right here."

He turned immediately, his hands tight on my ass as he lay me down on the hood of his car. The engine had been off for a while, so while it was still a little warm, it wasn't at all hot or unpleasant. I could feel the heat through the thin cotton t-shirt dress I had on.

Just as soon as I was sturdy, Javier sunk to the ground. My thighs spread before he even touched me, and I had to reach out and grip at the edges of the hood when I thought about the view he was getting down there. Those big hands worked my dress up even further until it was up around my waist. I kept my head up, looking down as he eyed my blue cotton panties.

Javier was silent as his lips brushed the insides of my thighs, and the soft, wet kisses he laid on my warm skin had me clenching my teeth in anticipation. He didn't spend a lot of time there, though. One of his thick fingers hooked around the gusset of my underwear and pulled it to the side. I felt myself clench as my bare pussy was exposed to the air. He touched me with his hand first, those fingertips brushing against the curls on my mons before trailing them down my slit.

"Fuck." He groaned when he pulled his fingers back to see them shining. "Look at that. Did I do this to you? Was it me who got you this wet, wife?"

My clit was throbbing. My opened panties and puffy, swollen lips had it so exposed. I needed him to take care of me, to put that frustrating mouth on my aching pussy and make me forget my own name.

"You know it was," I breathed. "You did this, so it's your job to make it better."

"Make it better?" He brought his head back down. His short facial hair brushed against the insides of my thighs and against my pussy. The feeling was rough, but it only served to make me drip even more. "What do you mean to make it better? Are you hurting here, Hannah? Is that pretty pussy aching? You need some relief?" He brushed his lips over my clit as he talked in what would have been a chaste kiss had he been on my mouth. "You want me to put my tongue on you here?"

"Jesus Christ." I lay my head back on the hood and tilted my face up at the sky. "Your ass is tryin' to kill me, I see."

"Nah." My hips canted up when his lips brushed against me this time, seeking the pleasure my body was longing for. "I just want you to use your words, wife. Remember when we talked about bein' open and honest about our feelins? Well, I want you to open up and tell me what you want, tell me everything you need me to do to please you the way you deserve to be pleased."

I could tell by his tone he wasn't going to let up, so I took two deep breaths to steady myself. One of my hands went into his hair, the dark, silky strands running through my fingers. Javier had his eyes on my cunt, not my face, so I tightened my grip just a little to grab his attention. His eyes were burning, the dark amber searing into mine.

"I want that tongue," I said softly. "I want you to lick me and stroke me and fill me. Make me come all over this handsome face. I want my legs to be weak afterward. I want you to eat this pussy so good I go to bed tonight and soak my sheets dreaming about your mouth on me."

"I think I can manage that." He ran his tongue over his lips.

"You think?" I raised an eyebrow at him.

He answered with a smirk as he leaned back down.

The first stroke of his tongue was enough to send a shock through me. He licked me long, from the space just above my clit to my clenching entrance, dipping inside briefly before doing it all over again. From there, I could barely keep track of where he went and what he did to me. An endless stream of shivers flowed up my back and settled into the base of my spine every time he suckled at my clit, or I felt his knuckles brush one of my lower lips from the way he gripped and pulled my underwear away from my body.

The atmosphere didn't do anything to make the scenario

less exciting. Javier and I were completely exposed. The house was relatively secluded and we weren't expecting anyone, but just the thought that anyone could happen by was more arousing than it should have been. It was almost completely silent except for the sounds of my moans, the grunts Javier let out every now and again, and the loud wet noises my pussy made. Even when braced against the hard hood of the car, I was incapable of feeling uncomfortable enough to ask Javier to move the party somewhere else. The feeling of his tongue, the air against my skin, and the warm hood on my back all combined in a way that made me close to tumbling over the edge.

"Fuck." I reached down and gripped his hair again. "Fuck, fuck, fuck. I'm coming!"

Javier's actions sped up. He focused his attention on my clit, and the suction of his lips was what finally did it. I stilled as I came, thighs twitching and belly dropping as he licked me through it.

I relaxed my thighs against the car a bit as I came down. He moved back just a little until his mouth wasn't touching me anymore. Javier had given me the best orgasm I'd had in a long time, but he didn't look completely satisfied.

"You think you can give me another one?" he asked, shocking me completely. But I had no interest in turning down the chance at another great orgasm.

"I think it's worth a shot."

I expected him to go about it the way he had before. Instead, his hands went to my hips and gripped the sides of my panties.

"Lift up for me a sec," he prompted as he worked them down.

He pushed the garment into one of my hands as his own worked up the backs of my thighs and clasped behind my knees, pushing my legs up towards my chest.

"Hold of these for me, Hannah."

I put my hands where his were in response, anchoring myself as he dived back into my pussy. This time, I wasn't on a hair-trigger. The first swipe of his tongue made me shiver, but it didn't make me shoot off. Javier was more relaxed too, his motions languid as he used both hands to spread me open for him to see and lick and fuck and please.

I was so swept up in the sensations, I didn't notice the sky darkening overhead. I didn't see the clouds becoming heavy with precipitation or that distinct ozone smell that always came along with rain. Javier had only just slid one finger into me when I felt the first few droplets on my skin.

The water was warm, but it still made me gasp in surprise. I knew Javier felt the droplets on his hair but he didn't stop— his fingers kept thrusting and his tongue kept sucking. Just as he continued, the rain did too. It wasn't a heavy fall but steady, more than a drizzle.

"Should…" I stuttered. "Should we go inside?"

Javier finally looked up at me, his lips pink and swollen and wet with my juices. "A little rain ain't never stopped me from gettin' my job done, Hannah."

He was right. It hadn't ever stopped me either. Anything outside of a severe thunderstorm or tornado warning never seemed to stop any type of show in our neck of the woods. If we could make shine in the rain, run errands in the rain, and play in the rain, I could get my pussy eaten in the rain. I figured the orgasm would be well worth the risk of a head cold.

"Go ahead and get back to work then." I pushed my legs even closer to my body.

Javier did exactly as instructed. I could feel my dress sticking to my body the wetter it got. I couldn't reach up and play with my nipples but they were as hard as steel, only more stimulated by the wetness that seeped through my thin bralette. Javier's dark hair looked even darker the more the water fell on him. He didn't pay it any attention and ate me through the loud splatters of rain against his car, through my loud gasps and moans, and through the soaking of his own clothes. I lasted longer than the time before, but not by too much.

This time when it happened, I couldn't be bothered to give him a warning. I hunkered down, tightening my hands behind my knees as my belly clenched and my heart thudded. He worked me through my orgasm with his mouth and fingers, but by the time my body calmed down, I was so hypersensitive I had no choice but to physically pull away.

He and I just looked at each other for a few seconds, our chests heaving. Then, Javier finally stood from his kneeling position on the ground.

"You goin' to carry me into the house?" I asked, leaning up on my elbows. "I don't think my legs are goin' to work for a while after that work you just put in."

"You?" He smiled. "I'm goin' to have to ice my knees later. I'm too damn old to be kneeling like that for so long."

"It was worth it though, huh?"

Javier leaned down and kissed me. I could taste myself on his lips and it made me deepen the kiss.

He pulled away and began to gather me up in his arms. My legs went around him immediately.

"So fuckin' worth it."

# CHAPTER 13

HANNAH

As much as I'd enjoyed my and Javier's little romp on the rain, it had thoroughly fucked up my hair. I was only a couple weeks into a fresh relaxer, but the humidity had my edges frizzy, and the water had the rest of my head looking like a hot mess. I was too lazy to try to fix it at home so the next day, I took the time to head over to Miss Sylvia's.

As small as it was, Harlan had two hair salons - both of which had a steady stream of business and neither of which knew anything about taking care of black hair. There weren't enough black people in town to truly justify the cost of paying rent or mortgage on a space for a regular salon, but Sylvia Williams found that her home beauty shop made her more than enough money to feed her family. So much so that over the years she'd gone from having customers lean over her kitchen sink to get their hair washed to turning her unfinished basement into a mini beauty shop—shampoo bowl and all.

Miss Sylvia had gone to beauty school and had made do with a curriculum that hadn't focused on hair like hers at all.

Twenty years later and she gave just as many relaxers as she did wash and gos. Even though the black men in town tended to go to a barbershop in Cumberland, some of the moms brought their little boys to her for their weekly lineups.

Every time I walked into her salon, I felt a sense of calmness and comfort that only ever came when I was in a space where I knew I'd be respected and understood. It was early afternoon on a Thursday so there were only a few people in the basement. Miss Sylvia looked up at me as soon as I hit the bottom step, her hands buried in someone's hair in the shampoo bowl.

"Jesus, girl. You ruined that flat iron quick, I see."

I sat down in one of the chairs on the far wall, my cheeks hot as hell at her observation. "I got caught in the rain, Miss Sylvia."

"Mmmhmm." She pursed her lips before looking back down at her work with a smirk.

Minutes later, I felt someone sit down next to me and looked up to see my sister. As soon as I'd told Nicole I'd planned to get my hair done, she'd invited herself along, claiming she needed to get her hair trimmed. I knew she didn't, not really. It was just her way of spending time with me. The past few weeks had been hectic as hell with the situation with the Wards and my new marriage. Both had made it hard to spend as much time with her as I normally did outside of the work we had to do together. It made me feel like shit. Nicole, Lex, and I were normally thick as thieves, had been since we were kids, and I'd been so distant lately.

"Where the hell did you get that?" I pointed to the beer in her hand in lieu of a regular greeting.

"Mike gave them to us upstairs." I was shocked to see Lex coming down the stairs, especially because she hated the beauty shop. My best friend had shoulder-length locs that she took care of herself.

Mike was Miss Sylvia's husband, a truck driver who was away for a couple of weeks out of the month. But when he was home, he always answered the front door for the people coming to see his wife.

Lex plopped down in the chair on the other side of me.

I pouted. "He didn't give me one."

Lex shrugged. "I guess that means he doesn't like you as much then."

"Bitch." I laughed. "What are you even doin' here?"

"I wanted to see you, but I didn't want to risk poppin' up at the house and walkin' in on you and your husband gettin' it in. So I let Nicki drag my ass down here." She took a long gulp of her beer.

"You could have come by." I rolled my eyes. "We ain't gettin' anything in...well, not really."

I couldn't decide whether that was a lie or not. I knew what Lex meant when she talked about "gettin' it in," and while Javier and I had definitely had a form of sex, we hadn't done *that* yet. I hoped the two women next to me would ignore the mumbled last words of my statement, but I knew them well enough to know they weren't going to.

"'Not really'?" My sister made air quotes with her fingers. "What does that mean?"

"It probably means somebody got licked or sucked or both," Lex responded.

I closed my eyes as I felt theirs bore into me. They weren't used to me being so hush-hush about my sexual exploits. Usually, I was more than willing to give details to a certain point, but I didn't want to do that with Javier. Our relationship and my feelings for him were both still new and uncertain. I didn't feel comfortable being as open as I normally would have been.

"*Anyway*." I drew out the word and listened as they giggled, taking that as my verification. "Javier ain't nearly in the front of my mind right now," I lied. "This shit with the Wards has me ready to pull my hair out."

They both winced.

"You introduced the Mezas to the kitchen crew yet?" Nicki asked.

"Not until tonight." I sighed. "I'm seriously dreading that shit."

I didn't at all regret the decision I'd made to let the Mezas use our workspace, but that didn't mean I wasn't apprehensive about it. I'd only just assured my people they wouldn't have to co-mingle with our rivals. I was hours away from telling them I'd completely broken that promise, and I really didn't want to see the disappointment and anger on their faces when I did.

"I think they'll understand why you did what you did," my sister said. "Just tell them you know Mama would have approved if she'd been here."

"Would she have?" I watched as Miss Sylvia combed the long wet hair back from her client's face to start cutting it.

I wasn't at all confident my mother would have made the choice I had. I'd grown up with the knowledge that the Mezas were our rivals, but I'd never really experienced that rivalry in any real way. Mama had—she'd been young when the Hawkins and Mezas couldn't be in the same square mile radius without trying to kill each other. Even outside of my mother's attempted kidnapping, there had been all kinds of fights and blow-ups.

My decision to join up with the Mezas to beat the Wards was one I felt she would have been behind completely. My decision to let them on our lands and into our kitchens, not so much.

Lex laid one of her hands on my knee, and I looked down at her black painted nails. "Miss Joy trusted you, Hannah. That's why she left all this responsibility to you instead of Clyde or Nicki."

"Hey!" My sister exclaimed in fake outrage.

Lex smiled but ignored her otherwise. "At the end of the day, it doesn't matter if she would have done the same thing or not. It's your time to make the decisions."

"She's right." My sister nodded. "I still think she would have approved, but when it comes down to it, you're our new leader. All those people on that mountain trust you to do what's best for us all, and if you're confident this is it, they better fall the fuck in line."

"Or what?" Lex asked, laughing at Nicole. "You goin' to go up there and beat their asses?"

My sister's chest puffed all out. "Shit, I might."

I couldn't help but laugh along with Lex at the thought. Body-wise, I looked more like my dad's side of the family, tall and full in pretty much every part of my body. Just like my paternal grandmother and aunts, I had a big ass and a stomach that refused to be hidden. Lex, on the other hand, was all Hawkins. She was a good head shorter than me and very thin.

Neither of us had been fighters as kids or adults, but Nicki was notoriously bad at it. I'd never let her go full steam ahead at anybody in my defense just to watch her get stomped out, but it was cute she'd suggested it.

I leaned over and kissed her on the cheek. "I don't think it'll come to that." I chuckled. "But thank you."

Miss Sylvia was putting her client under one of two hairdryers in the room when she called out to me to get my butt in the shampoo chair.

I stood, noting that Lex and Nicki settled further into their chairs.

"Are y'all really about to stay here the whole time?" I asked.

"Yup." Lex gulped down the rest of her beer and sat it on the ground. "We're stayin' until you tell us exactly what that 'not really' meant earlier."

I snorted. "You better get used to that chair then because you're goin' to be waitin' on that forever."

"This is it." I parked my car on a dirt patch on the side of Black Mountain, looked in my rearview mirror to see the black car behind me, and motioned out of my window for it to stop.

The sun had only just begun setting, so the light blue sky still had plenty of light. I hoped the prolonged spring daylight would persist long enough for us to finish the meeting. I'd never admit it out loud, not even to myself, but I hated being on the mountain after dark. It didn't matter that I knew the land like the back of my hand. It was still creepy as hell.

Javier and I exited the car and stood by as we waited for Alma and Benicio to join us. I looked in the canvas bag I had strapped across my body, took out one of the flashlights, and handed it over to Alma. "Here. You might need this later."

She stared into the woods with her brows drawn. "How long is the walk-up?"

"Not far at all. A little under a mile and we've made our own little trail if you kn n husband. "You ready?"

We were off then, disappearing into the thick covering of wilderness. We stayed relatively quiet as I led the way, the only real sounds the loud chirping of crickets and the sound of our feet hitting the earth underneath us repeatedly. The brush of trees was thick and green b ut plenty of light still peeked through, making the flashlights obsolete in the early evening.

We made it to the kitchen in about fifteen minutes, and it was buzzing with people. Some of them were standing around while others were obviously finishing up for the day.

Almost like we were in a movie, the large room quieted

down as soon as we entered, eyes flicking from me to the family standing with me and then back to me again.

"Hey y'all," I greeted.

I didn't want to make a show out of the announcement. I was already anxious enough about the whole ordeal, so I didn't want to draw it out either. Whatever my people were about to throw at me, I wanted them to go ahead and get it over with.

"I've got some news, so I need y'all to come on and gather around here."

I paused as they did what I asked. My eyes flickered over the twenty or so faces. I noticed Miss Donna and her guys near the back, all four of them with their eyes hard and their arms crossed.

I swallowed harshly. "I'm sure you know who these people are, but I'll introduce them anyway," I almost winced at having to project my voice so much. "This is Javier, Alma, and Benicio Meza."

I heard a few grumbles throughout the crowd but kept going.

"Now, the last time I made an announcement about them I was tellin' y'all that I'd be workin' with them to take care of the bastards who shot Bobby. And after that, I was assurin' you that you wouldn't have to rehash any bad blood by workin' with them too closely."

I swallowed and looked over at Javier. He was next to me but had kept a little bit of distance, making sure not to touch me when we were in such a tense situation.

"Well, I was wrong about that." The murmurs of displeasure grew louder, so I forced myself to speak louder. "I know y'all already know about the Wards settin' the Meza's whole operation on fire. They lost everything. *Everything.* So, I've decided to let them use our resources temporarily. Just until they get back on their feet."

My people weren't happy with the announcement. I definitely hadn't expected them to be, but I'd somehow underestimated how much seeing their anger would hurt me. My chest panged and clenched because of it. I was doing the right thing, the thing that made the most sense to me, but fuck if I didn't still feel like I'd just handed down a major betrayal to the people who counted on me.

"Wait a minute," Lee Bryant called out from his standing place near the front of the small crowd. "Where's Clyde? Ain't no way he agreed to this."

"Clyde is still in Louisville takin' care of his aunt Clara," I answered. "But he and I talked about this for a long time and he agreed with me that it's for the best. He knows just as well as I do that y'all are grown enough to set aside your differences for a little bit, especially when we have so much at stake."

Lee didn't want to hear it. His pale brown cheeks were ruddy with anger. "So that's how things are goin' to be now? You're with them over there," he pointed to the three people standing next to me, "and we don't have nobody on our side over here."

"Miss Joy would have never allowed them in our place like this," Amma Shaw joined in. "She's probably rollin' over in her grave at the thought of it."

"My mama was cremated," I snapped. "She ain't got no grave to roll around in."

Hard as it was to hear, I was fine with letting them voice their displeasure. Their feelings were justified and as their leader, it was my job to take them into concern, even if my decision wasn't going to change. I drew the line at the mention of my mother though. I could sit around all day and speculate about how disappointed and angry Mama would have been at me, but I wasn't about to let somebody else do it. Especially not someone who couldn't fully empathize with the situation I was in.

"You can be as mad as you want Ms. Shaw." I made sure to keep my voice even, being mindful I was still speaking to someone two decades my senior. "But you leave her out of this. She ain't here. She doesn't have to make these decisions, I do."

The woman had the good sense to look ashamed, so I backed off. I looked around the room, making sure to take in each and every face staring at me.

"The Meza's crew won't be here during the day anyway." I looked over at Javier and he sent me a wink. It wasn't meant to be sexy, but the silent support gave me a little more confidence. "Y'all are normally out of here by nine, but I'm goin' to ask that you be packed up by eight for a little while. That's when they'll come in every day. The only time you have to see each other is when you're leavin' and they're comin' in. If you ain't good with that arrangement, you're free to go."

The collective eyes of the group widened at the suggestion.

"I don't want that. No matter how mad y'all are at me, y'all are my family. But I'm not about to force y'all to stay here out of a false sense of loyalty. If the thought of workin' with the Mezas eats you up inside that much, I'm willin' to let you go. You'll have your normal pay and my blessin'."

I held my breath, waiting for someone to walk out. Losing one of these people would feel like losing a limb. It didn't matter that none of them had my last name—they were my family. The closest and most loving family anyone could ever dream of, even when they were steaming mad at me.

"We ain't goin' anywhere," Amma spoke up. Her jaw was still clenched but her face was significantly less angry. "We never let anybody run us off this damn mountain and we ain't about to start now. Not with them rich bastards or these regular bastards."

"Miss Amma," I scolded, even among the laughter.

I looked over at the Mezas again to see Benicio and Alma smirking and Javier biting back a smile of my own. I waved Benicio over to me.

"I want to thank you, folks," he said after clearing his throat. "We know this change can't be easy for y'all, but I appreciate it anyway. Like Hannah said, we're goin' to make sure we stay out of y'alls hair as much as possible. I'm goin' to have a chat with my people and make sure they know to be on their best behavior while they're in your space."

"Y'all better heed that warning too," I interrupted. "I'm not tryin' to get called up here to break up fights between my elders. As long as we all keep it cool, this will go smooth."

I ran my tongue over my lips, finally feeling calm. Things

had gone relatively well, considering, and I'd been expecting the worst. I was ecstatic that none of my fatalistic nightmare scenarios had come true.

"The Mezas are comin' in tomorrow night, so make sure everything is clean and prepared for them at the end of the day. They'll do the same for you at the end of their shift." I leaned up on my toes to look for Donna. "Miss Donna, make sure you're properly labelin' the liquor barrels so we know how many more runs through the still they need since we can't keep the shine in there overnight anymore."

She was little, so I couldn't see her well over the other tall people, but I heard her agree.

"Anybody got anything else to add?" I looked around. "If not, we can all get out of here. I'm sure everybody has somethin' to do tonight."

I stayed put for a little while longer, waiting for someone to come up to me with a question or concern as people started filing out of the kitchen. When no one did, I wasn't sure whether to feel glad or offended.

As we trekked back through the woods, flashlights in hand, I knew a weight had been lifted off my shoulders. Something else was left in its place—pride, or relief, or confidence. Maybe all three. I couldn't fully place it, but it had me grinning by the time I was standing by my car.

"Hey." Javier wrapped an arm around my waist and pulled me to him. "I'm goin' to catch a ride back with Mami and Pop. I've got a couple hours 'til we need to be over at the Wards."

My smile was knocked off my face immediately when I

remembered what was about to go down. Javier and two other guys were about to kidnap the Ward brothers. We knew they didn't have any guards or real protection, but the situation was still scary. I didn't want anything bad to happen to any of them, but the thought of Javier getting killed or worse made me clutch onto him harder.

"Okay." I nodded, trying to hide the quiver in my voice with a cough. "Just...just be careful. Don't get killed."

Javier leaned down and kissed me, a soft, dry kiss that made me feel warm inside.

"Make sure you come home to me, little husband."

He groaned playfully at the name.

"I'll leave you if you don't."

He didn't answer me verbally, but he gave me another kiss that almost lifted me off my feet before he stepped back.

He stood next to my car, watching and waiting until I was inside with the doors locked and my seatbelt on before he joined his parents.

# CHAPTER 14

JAVIER

I brought Sam and Cameron with me—Cameron because he was just as tall as me and bulkier, easily able to wrangle the relatively skinny Ward brothers, and Sam because the kid always acted like he was behind the wheel of a Formula One race car anytime he got his foot on a pedal.

We approached the Ward mansion at a little after one in the morning. Cam and Sam, who'd already been watching the property, had assured me there were no cameras outside, but we weren't sure about the inside the place so we all wore black ski masks just in case. We knew both brothers kept their bedrooms on the ground floor and tended to keep their curtains open at all hours of the day and night. They had a false sense of security, one that told them our mountains were so quiet, serene, and docile they could leave the sliding doors of their big ass house unlocked every night and not come to any harm.

The plan was to break in through the back, quietly make our way to the front of the house where the bedrooms were, and grab each brother up individually, at the same time. We'd brought zipties to bind their hands and feet and duct tape for their mouths. Cameron had even gotten a couple of cheap sleep masks at the dollar store so we could keep them from seeing where we were taking them.

It seemed like a pretty solid plan, even if we had come up with it in under a day. I was still nervous as hell, though. The closest I'd gotten to kidnapping somebody was when me and a few other guys stole my cousin Danny out his bed in the middle of the night for a surprise bachelor party. He'd come around as the night went on, but he hadn't taken it well at first. I'd come out of the scenario with a black eye and a promise to myself to never do any dumb shit like that again.

I guessed it would just be one of many in a long list of promises I would break in my life.

By the time I was slowly sliding the glass door open, my heart was racing. I could feel my pulse making the vein in my neck twitch. Cameron and I walked through the kitchen, making sure our shoes didn't slap too hard on the marble floors. There were dishes piled up in the sink, and the huge island in the center of the room was covered in enough pizza boxes to feed an entire battalion.

I couldn't help but stop when we got to the living room. The ceilings were ridiculously high, and the whole of my little house in Cumberland could have probably fit in the huge space. I turned my nose up a bit as I looked at the gold trimmings and expensive furniture. It was too damn much for one family. I didn't understand what they needed with so much space, why they needed so much shit. I could have hocked everything in there and fed at least five families in town for months with the money.

I hated that these assholes were living in such luxury while there were people miles away who still had trouble getting running water in their homes. The sight of so much needless bullshit only made me dislike them even more.

Cameron moved in front of me as he led the way to the hallway I assumed held the bedrooms. Once we were standing in the middle of the hall, he stopped and pointed to himself, and then pointed to the room at the end of the hall. Then he pointed to me and pointed to a room to my right. I nodded, signifying I understood him as my heart pounded even faster.

As much as I hated the giant mansion, I was grateful as hell for the new build. The impeccably laid hardwood floors and greased door hinges made sure I made virtually no noise as I walked over to Carver who was sleeping in the bed.

I pulled a roll of duct tape out of one of the deep pockets in the cargo pants I wore and pulled some tape as quietly as possible before ripping it with my teeth. The first thing I did was slap it on top of his mouth, causing him to wake up immediately. Carver's eyes were wide and filled with terror as he flopped around, trying to scream behind the tape. I was faster than him, pulling him up out of bed by the front of his shirt and spinning him until his back was to me. I slapped two zipties on him, one around his wrists and another around his forearms before I turned him back around and pushed him on the bed. His feet were bare, which made putting a tie around them easy.

He was still squirming by the time I leaned a knee down on the bed, smiled down at him, and lifted my mask.

"Remember me, Carver?"

He nodded.

"Good." I flicked his forehead two times. "I want you to know who's responsible for doin' this to you."

I looked behind me when I heard footsteps in the doorway behind me. Cam was standing with Avery slung over his shoulder, and I could tell the dude was knocked out.

He shrugged when I raised my eyebrows at him.

"He wouldn't stop fuckin' movin' around, man."

I looked down to see the Carver still moving like hell, trying to free himself. I didn't give my actions a second thought as I cold cocked him right in the face. It was strong enough to keep him out for the few minutes it would take to get to the car and give him a nasty black eye when he woke up. A part of me wanted to keep hitting, to fuck his face all the way up in payback for what he and his family had done, but I figured we had plenty of time for that later.

I moved the ski mask back down over my face and hefted the dude up, groaning a bit as his weight settled on my shoulder.

"Don't forget to grab his phone," Cam called. "We'll need to make sure the location tracker is off, but we're goin' to need the numbers on it to get in contact with his old man."

After I grabbed the device off the bedside table, we booked it out of the front door and towards where Sam had the SUV parked in the circular driveway. Neither of us was running at full speed, and I could hear both of us panting as we lugged the two dead weights.

"We good?" Sam looked at us as we loaded our cargo into the very back and climbed in ourselves.

"Let's go," I said, my breath still lost.

The farther we got from the Ward mansion, the lighter I felt. I'd just done something heinous as hell, kidnapped two human beings from their beds and left them scared and in pain while I laughed at their plight. I probably should have felt ashamed or something even remotely close to remorseful, but I didn't.

Images of Hannah's runner bleeding out behind the wheel of his truck and of my family's entire life being burned to the ground kept flashing through my mind. The day before, I'd told Hannah and my parents we needed to hit the Wards hard, put some goddamn fear in their bones. We weren't going to kill or seriously maim those two assholes, but I did plan to do whatever it took just short of that to show them we had no intention of being fucked with or fucked over.

My family owned a few different pieces of land in Harlan County. When the moonshining business had first started taking off for my great grandfather, he'd used a lot of the money to buy up property. He'd explained that back then, everybody said owning your own land was a crucial part of achieving the American Dream. Time had proved it hadn't been, but my father had always refused to sell the land.

Most of it was empty, just multiple acres of overgrown grass and untended trees, but one specific plot was the perfect place to house a couple of hostages. It was nearly an hour north of Cumberland in an area that had so little people, it couldn't even be classified as a town.

There had been an old barn on the property when my grandfather bought it. Instead of tearing it down, he'd fixed it up a bit and used it to hold liquor stores during times when prohibition crackdowns really ramped up.

The barn was huge, all dark wood that made it hard to spot during the nighttime unless you were looking for it. Three guys were waiting for us when we pulled up, one who normally worked with Cameron as a runner for the Hawkins and two men who worked as stillers for my family. The brothers were wide awake by the time we arrived at the spot, but they were still and quiet. I assumed they'd realized there was no way out of the trouble they'd found themselves in.

The six of us unloaded Carver and Avery from the SUV and tied them to two chairs in the middle of the barn. I stood back and watched as the masks were taken off their faces, their eyes widening as they took in their surroundings. Aside from a few lights which hung from the high ceiling, it was pretty much empty. There were no beds, no bathrooms, and damn sure no marble-floored kitchens.

I didn't take my mask off until I saw my father come into the barn. He walked straight past me and the other guys to stand right in front of Carver Ward. Pop ripped the duct tape off of the man's mouth, and we all listened as he hissed loudly in pain.

"You fuckin—"

Pop grabbed Carver's face up in his hand, stopping the man before he could get his words out fully. "If you don't want me to call my son over here to beat you black and blue, you'll watch that mouth of yours, little boy."

My father pointed to where I stood a few feet away with my arms crossed. Carver looked over at me, and I smiled wide when his eyes locked with mine. I hadn't been in a fight in years, but I was more than willing to beat some ass the second my father gave the go-ahead.

He didn't get the chance, though, because the coward nodded his head in agreement and Pop released his face. Then, he moved over to Avery and ripped the tape from his mouth.

"I'm not goin' to drag this damn thing out," Pop said. "You two know why you're here."

"I'm not sure we do," Carver said boldly.

"Oh, we want to play dumb?"

Carver shrugged.

"All right then," Pop said with a shrug of his own. "I'm a father so I know when it's time to take a step back and leave children to reflect on their actions." He turned around and started walking towards the door. "We'll give you a few days to see if you're ready to act like adults and own your shit. In the meantime," he pointed to the two stillers who'd met us when we arrived, "Angel and George will take care of you. Make sure you stay put, nice and cozy, until we get back."

My father practically had to drag me by the collar of my T-shirt to get me out of the barn.

"Pop?" I questioned. "That's it?"

"It's not goin' to be that easy, Javier. We need to play the long game. They might be cowards, but they ain't givin' up their father that quick. We'll let them eat bologna sandwiches on stale bread and shit in holes in the woods for a few days first. Let them get scared and desperate. Then we'll start gettin' to what we really want."

I wanted to run back in there and do the exact opposite. I wanted to go back into that barn and beat Carver's smug ass until he was crying at my father's feet and apologizing for what he'd done to us. I'd never been much of a hothead, but the Wards were bringing it out in me in a way that made me feel things so foreign, I couldn't even name them. My father was right and I knew it. As keyed and heated up as I felt, I needed to follow his orders as both my leader and my Pop and back the fuck off.

"Okay." It was the only thing I could manage.

Pop reached out and clasped my shoulder, squeezing it and then drawing me in for a hug. "Don't worry, mijo." He spoke quietly in my ear, using the endearment he only used when he knew I was fucked up emotionally. "They ain't goin' to win. They don't even have a chance anymore. Not after this."

# CHAPTER 15

JAVIER

It took me over an hour to get back home. Even after dropping both Sam and Cam back off at their cars at my parents' place in Cumberland, and making my way to Harlan, I still hadn't calmed down completely. I was buzzing with adrenaline that made my skin itch.

I opened the door quietly, planning to make a beeline towards the little liquor cart Hannah kept in the kitchen. I knew she had a fresh bottle of Hawkins bourbon sitting right in front, and I hoped the corn liquor would help mellow me out a bit.

My wife stopped me in my tracks, though. I hadn't even noticed the light through the front window but she was sitting up on the couch when I walked in, wide awake as she worked a stick through a piece of fabric in her lap. She looked beautiful, obviously dressed for bed with her hair already wrapped and her brown skin glowing. I wanted to go over there and kiss her.

"You knit?" It was the only thing I could get out at the moment.

"Crochet." She sat the blue square aside. "My granny taught me. I only do it when I'm too nervous to focus on anythin' else or I can't sleep."

"What do you have to be nervous about?"

She gave me a dry look.

"I told you I'd be back," I offered.

Even when I was completely on edge, I didn't want Hannah to feel the same. It was nearing four in the morning and just the thought of her waiting up for me to come home for hours on end added a little bit of lightness to my dark mood.

Hannah walked over to me, her eyes diligently searching my face. "What's wrong? It didn't go well."

"Nah, it went fine. We got both of them to the spot, but Pop wants us to wait a few days to spook them some more."

"And you don't want that?" she asked slowly.

"It ain't that." She reached out and ran a hand from my shoulder down my arm until she was clutching one of my biceps. "I just..."

I didn't know how to properly express what I was feeling to her. Not out of shame or because I was being guarded, but because I couldn't get a real handle on it to nail it down. All I knew was I couldn't stop gritting my teeth, and my chest felt like it was seconds from caving in on my rib cage.

"You just wanted your payback," she said. "And you were expectin' to get it tonight and now that you didn't, your emotions and body are still tryin' to catch up with what you already know logically."

I nodded. Her description sounded pretty spot on.

Hannah moved in closer. "Well, what do you do when you're normally worked up? How do you get it out?"

"I try not to let myself get there," I answered. "Not a lot of things can do this to me."

"Okay, but there's got to be times when you need some kind of release when your emotions get to be too much." She raised her eyebrows. "Everybody has somethin'."

"Normally I just beat off." It wasn't a joke, but I presented it as one.

"So, jerking off is your crocheting then?"

The chuckle was forced out of me. "Yeah, that sounds about right."

"So there you go, then. You'll just have to jerk off." Hannah smiled up at me like she was talking about something as small as the weather and not me masturbating.

"Uh, all right. I'll go do that then…"

Hannah tucked her thumb underneath the arm of my T-shirt and rubbed my skin there. "Maybe since we both obviously need to take the edge off, we can do it together." The little smile on her face was just as enticing as her words.

"Yes," I said a little too quickly. "Shit, yes."

Hannah bit down on her full bottom lip. Her eyes had become a little heavier. "Go take a shower and meet me in my room after," she said before she walked away from me and up the stairs.

It took everything in me not to rush through my shower in an overeager attempt to join Hannah.

I took my time scrubbing my body, my dick already hard as I ran a cloth over myself, trying to get rid of the sweat and stress of the day. I spent a good nearly twenty minutes under the hot water, but I rushed through the rest of my nighttime ritual, forgoing boxers and a shirt for a pair of flannel pajama pants. I gave myself a lookover in the mirror, noting how impossible it would be for Hannah not to notice how hard I was.

Nervous wasn't the word I would use to describe how I felt in the moment. Being with Hannah always had a way of calming me, and even just the thought of her had made some of that itchy feeling underneath my skin fade. But I felt keyed up in a different way, in the same way I'd felt when I'd gone down on her the day before. Blood rushed through me and thoughts of her made my head race as they consumed me. Hours after I'd had my first and second taste of her, Hannah had been asleep in her room, and I'd jerked my dick with the flavor of her still on my lips, my desire for her burning hot and strong.

I knocked on her door, waiting for her verbal go-ahead before I went in. Hannah was sitting on a towel in the middle of her bed wearing the same white tank top she'd had on earlier, her same headscarf, and a pair of dark panties that rose up a bit and sat high on her hips and belly. I could see her dark nipples through the fabric of her top and couldn't help but think about how I still hadn't gotten the chance to see them fully, let alone get my hands and mouth on them.

"Sit right there." She pointed to a soft chair that had obviously been pulled from the corner to sit inches from the bed.

Once I was seated, she fluffed her pillows up against her headboard and leaned her back against it. I had an unobstructed view of her from my place in the chair. She sat with her legs bent at the knees and her feet on the bed, and I had a perfect showing of her big pretty legs spread just a little bit. My mouth watered at the sight of her plump pussy lips pressing tight against the crotch of her panties.

She was incredible, too beautiful for words to describe. Even if there'd been words, I doubted I'd ever be eloquent enough to put a voice to them.

"How do you normally do this?" she asked. "Do you watch porn?"

"Sometimes," I said.

I hadn't really since I'd moved into the Hawkins house. I hated how those little earphones felt, and I knew the walls in the house were thin and didn't want to risk making Hannah feel uncomfortable.

"Lately, my own imagination has been enough."

"Oh?" She smiled and looked at me under those hooded eyes. "What have you been thinkin' about?"

"You," I said simply. "I think about you."

"Tell me." It was technically a demand, but it came from her lips sounding like a plea.

My dick was so hard it had was pressed upwards against my body. I went to tuck the head into the waist of my pants when I saw Hannah looking. She blinked slowly, her face masked as she eyed me, so I left it alone, letting my hardness tent my pajama pants. If we actually did what she'd suggested downstairs, it wouldn't be in there for long anyway.

"I want to hear one of the fantasies you have about me." Her voice was soft and husky.

Her request should have been easy, but searching through my head, I came across what must have been a million scenarios I'd made up about fucking her. I decided to go with the most recent.

"Last night, it took everythin' in me to brush my teeth before I went to bed because I could still taste your pussy and I didn't want it to go away. I didn't know when I was goin' to get to have you next so, before I got ready for bed, I decided that I wanted to come with you still on my lips."

Hannah's fingers were trailing across her chest, the unpainted nails dragging every now and again. I wanted to lick her collar bones, kiss all over her sweet-smelling neck.

"I was thinkin' about what would have happened in that hotel room in Nashville if we'd been ready for all that then." I reached down to adjust myself, squeezing the base of my dick a bit through my pants to try and calm him down.

"Can I see you, Javier?" Hannah sat up a little straighter. "Can you take it out?"

The woman probably could have asked me to jump off the roof of her house at the moment, and I would have been inclined to do it. Letting her see my dick was something I was more than happy to oblige her with.

I smiled at the soft, little moan she let out when I pulled my pants down some and let my cock show.

She put her hands on her hips, working her panties down

and off her body. Her legs spread more and I could see her bare to me. Her pussy was swollen and so wet, I could see the insides of her thighs shining.

Hannah reached over into her bedside table and pulled a couple things out. She tossed something across the bed at me —a small bottle of lube.

"That's for you." She held up the other thing with a smile. "This is for me."

It was a vibrator—or maybe a just a dildo. I couldn't fully tell. But it was long and black and curved and I knew immediately there were very few things in the world I wanted more than to watch her fuck herself with it.

"Keep goin' please." Hannah languidly rubbed the toy against her lips. "I want to hear more about what you would have done to me in that hotel room."

"I meant what I said about you lookin' fine as hell that night." As I talked, I poured some of the lube into my hand, slicking it up before I wrapped my fingers around my dick. Normally, I just used whatever lotion I had closest to me, sometimes even spit. It felt so incredible that I went silent for a few moments. When I spoke again, my voice was gruff. "You spent our time at the speakeasy all up against me. The way your legs looked in that dress, that pretty dark lipstick you had on, that gorgeous ass rubbin' against my dick while we danced, everythin' about you had me wired and ready to fuck."

Hannah opened her thighs a little more and pushed the toy inside herself. Her head tilted back as she shuddered at the feeling. I could see goosebumps on the inside of her thighs, and I wanted to run my fingers over them. Instead, I stroked myself a little faster, having no shame about working myself over the way I normally did when I was alone.

"If things had been different, you would have fucked me that night?" She slowly thrust the toy in and out of herself.

"I would have tried to consume you, wife. I would have gotten you out of that pretty dress, stripped you down until you were completely bare for me, and then had you sit on my face."

She pulled the toy out of her and it came to life with the press of a button. She rubbed it over her clit, and back and forth down her slit as she stared over at me with darkly blown pupils. "You do have a very rideable face."

She seemed to like the idea.

"I would have kept you up there for as long as you could take it." I ran my thumb over the head of my dick. The sensitivity made me breathe a little faster. "Then, when you were shaking and soaking from the pleasure of it, I would have fed you my dick."

Hannah released a low humming sound. "I've thought about you fuckin' my face more than a few times. Thought about makin' you breathless as I worked you over. Thought about you cryin' out as I took those balls in my mouth."

Her confession had me reaching down to tug at said balls, squeezing them just hard enough to make myself moan.

"Where would you have come, Javier?" She was back to fucking herself, her body clutching the vibrating toy as she slid it in and out of her juicy cunt. "In my mouth? On my face?"

I shook my head. "Nah, I would have pulled you off me before I came. That face of yours would look beautiful covered in my come, but I wouldn't have wanted to shoot off so fast. I'd have wanted to get inside you first."

"And how would you have fucked me, Javier?"

Every time she said my name like that, all breathy and low, my thoughts scattered for a few seconds. I doubted she knew it, but Hannah was dangerously close to having me wrapped around all ten of her fingers. Toes too, if I was being honest. It had been unexpected as hell, but not at all unwelcome, just like me finding myself in her bedroom getting myself off to the sight and sound of her.

"I would have had you on your knees, first. Those thighs spread wide and your back arched. I already know you would have fucked me back just as good as I gave." I was getting close. I could feel the heat rising in my balls as I slid my hand up and down myself faster.

I could see the telltale signs in Hannah too. Her thighs were quivering a little and the wet sounds her pussy made were just as loud as her little moans and groans.

"I would have watched as that ass bounced off me, diggin' as deep into you as I could." The warm feeling in my balls rose into my shaft, my strokes tugging and circling as I imagined my hand was Hannah's hot, wet pussy. "You like it fast or slow, wife?"

"Both," she moaned. "Depends on the situation, but I would have wanted you to fuck me fast then."

"Fast, with my hands on your hips, fillin' you up over and

over while you dripped down your thighs and on those white sheets."

"Oh, fuck!" Hannah was pounding herself, her ass writhing on the bed as she used one hand to trust and another to rub her clit. "You want to see somethin', Javier? See what I would have done all over your dick if you'd fucked me in that hotel room?"

"Show me, baby." I couldn't take my eyes off of the space between her thighs. "Show me how you would have come all over my dick."

She only got three more thrusts in and out before she was off. The vibrator was forced out of her, lightly thrown on the bed next to her as her orgasm made her arch off the bed. She gushed, literally, splashes of the clear liquid rushing from her swollen pussy. There was a lot of it, landing all over her thighs and on the towel below her. Hannah was silent as she came, but just when I thought she was done, she stuck a couple fingers back into herself then pulled them out, smacking her clit as more came.

The moan that left me was in response to her orgasm just as it was to my own. My own come spilled fast, running all over my fist and my stomach, the force even leaving a bit on my chest. I was left breathing hard, my body going slightly numb as my dick still puffed up even after I'd finished spilling over.

"Fuck, that was sexy," Hannah breathed, her legs still spread wide as she lay on her bed. "I think I'm goin' to be obsessed with watchin' you come now."

"You?" I asked, my eyes wide. "Are you kiddin' me? I had

no idea you could squirt. Now, I'm goin' to want to see that shit all the time."

"It takes some special technique to learn how to make me do it." She chuckled.

"I'll learn whatever the hell I need to in order to make you do that on my face as often as possible." I was dead serious.

"I'll teach you." She sat up and I could see the sexy fold of her stomach through her tank top.

I stood, went around to the side of the bed she was on, and leaned down to brush my lips against hers. My dick was still half-hard against my thigh as I kissed her, the feeling of her hot mouth and soft tongue against mine making my spine tingle.

"Let's go clean up," I said softly against her mouth, before helping her up.

We gathered her wet towel and threw it in the hamper in the bathroom before washing ourselves up.

Once we were both done, Hannah turned to me, her soft hands touching the dusting of hair in the middle of my chest. "Will you sleep with me tonight?" she asked softly. "In my bed."

My hand went to her face, cupping the apple of her cheek. I had to swallow down emotion in order to stop myself from saying something ridiculous. From telling her how incredible she was, how happy she'd already made me, or how I would forever be grateful she was even willing to consider spending the rest of her life with me. I didn't know if Hannah would want to hear those things or if I was willing to say them out loud yet, so I just smiled at her.

JODIE SLAUGHTER

"Only if you let me hold you as I did in Nashville."

She led me back into her room, sliding into the left side of the bed. Her back was to me as I got in behind her. I brought my arm around her front, resting my open palm against her stomach while my hips pressed up against her ass.

"Just like Nashville," I said softly into the back of her neck after she'd turned the lamp off.

"Better than Nashville," Hannah replied as she interlocked our fingers.

# CHAPTER 16

HANNAH

I'd let Benicio take the lead when it came to kidnapping the Ward brothers. We both had ample reason to hate the bastards, but the Mezas had the space to hold them, the people to spare to make sure it went off smoothly, and the brain space to add something else to their plate. I didn't have any of those things. My own people were still sore about having to work with the Mezas, so I didn't feel comfortable putting more than a few of them on the kidnapping job. We certainly didn't have any land to spare, and I had a million things to get done.

So, after the third day of waiting for Benicio's go-ahead to approach the brothers again with no answer, I left town completely. I still needed to buy a new still and I wanted to check in on Clyde, see how he and his Aunt Clara were faring and talk to him about what was going on back home.

I traded my car for Nicole's truck for the day, knowing I'd need something big to lug the new copper still across the state. The drive to Louisville was almost four hours long, and Javier wouldn't let me leave in the morning before fussing over me. We'd woken up early and he'd made me my favorite breakfast sandwich—crispy bacon, a fried egg white, and cheddar cheese on an English muffin. Then he'd checked the tires on Nicole's truck, mumbling something about how I'd have to go through Laurel County and their fucked up roads were like to make me blow one out. The man had even sent me off with a little tote bag of snacks so I wouldn't have to stop if I got hungry along the way.

Maybe I should have told him to calm down, let him know I was driving a few hours not taking a trip across the ocean, and that it was a drive I'd made countless times since I was a kid. I said none of that, though, because I was too caught up in how fucking sweet he was. The sight of my big, gruff-looking husband pleading with me to call him if anything happened to go wrong had me grinning long after I'd driven away from him.

I went to *Louisville Copper & Brass Company* first. I was waiting outside at nine, ready to go in the second they opened. We'd gotten our last set of stills from them and the owner, Teddy, knew Clyde. The process of buying the equipment was pretty easy. I knew exactly the one I wanted, was able to pick it and pay for it quickly and had a few of the guys working there load it into my truck in under ten minutes. I made sure the still was strapped down and covered with the plastic truck bed topper to avoid any trouble as I made my way through the rural counties on the way home. My name may have meant something in Appalachia, but to anyone anywhere else I would have just looked like any other criminal shiner. The very last thing I needed was to draw suspicion from some overeager cop.

Clyde's aunt was staying in the university's hospital in downtown Louisville. I met Clyde in the lobby after almost getting lost in the parking garage.

He grabbed me up as soon as he saw me, the smell of his cologne making me feel comforted immediately. "You got no idea how good it is to see you, girl."

He had only been away from home for about a week, but I could feel the stress pouring out of him. He had bags under his eyes, his dark brown skin bruised and shadowed around the same area. Clyde always kept a clean-shaven face so the stubble that had grown on his cheeks and chin was a clear sign he hadn't been taking care of himself.

"Jesus, Clyde." I clutched at him, hating seeing him so clearly distressed. "You didn't even look this bad when Mama passed."

I didn't mean it as an insult but an observation. I was lucky he knew me well enough that my words didn't come as insensitively as they would have with anyone else.

"I didn't have to watch your mama die." He ran a hand over his bald head.

He was right. Mama had gone quickly and unexpectedly. By the time anyone had realized something was wrong, she'd already been close to the brink. By the time Nicole and I had gotten to the hospital, she'd been gone for good. It was a tragic incident, one that had been impossible to truly prepare for. As difficult as it was, I found myself grateful she hadn't had to suffer long.

Clyde led me up to his aunt's room in the oncology ward. Her room was nice. She had a bed that resembled one that would have been in an actual house. There were a couple comfortable-looking couches and a medium-sized flat-screened television. She even had a view of the city through her window.

When we got in, she was sleeping, her small body curled up on her side as she burrowed into her white sheets. I'd never met the woman, but her relation to Clyde meant I loved her. Besides, seeing anyone suffering so obviously was heart-breaking.

"I used my life's savings to pay for this room for her," Clyde said, sitting down on one of the couches. "I didn't really know her that well, but she doesn't have anybody else."

"What does she have?" I sat down next to him.

"Pancreatic cancer, metastatic stage four. It's already spread to her lungs and breasts. Doctors say she's got six months, if that."

"Is there anything we can do?" I reached out and took his hand. "We can contribute to the cost of the room for her."

He shook his head back and forth. "No, you don't need to do all that."

"Remember Mama always tellin' you to stop bein' so stubborn and accept help?" I tried to lighten things up a little by giving him a small smile. "It's time to take that advice."

Clyde looked at me, his eyes shining with tears.

"Please." I swallowed back some tears of my own.

He sighed. "All right."

I thanked him with a hug, pretending not to notice when I felt a couple of tears soak through the shoulder of my T-shirt.

"How are things goin' in the kitchens?" he asked as we pulled away. "They gettin' along?"

The subject made me rub my fingers against my temples. "I don't know about gettin' along, but they haven't killed each other yet. They are constantly complainin', though. They need you out there to straighten them up."

Clyde laughed, and I could tell it was genuine when I saw his eyes crinkle at the sides. "I'll be there soon to put some fear back in them."

"You better. I think they're way more scared of you than they could ever be of me." That was also the truth. I may have been their leader, but Clyde was the irreplaceable, essential glue that kept us together.

"'Cause they know I'm always ready to stomp out anybody who steps to my girl." He raised my hand up to lay a fatherly kiss on the back. "Speakin' of, how are things goin' with that husband of yours?"

My face got hot immediately. It was soon, so fucking soon, but things with Javier were going well. Much better than I'd ever expected, actually. We still hadn't had sex, and I wasn't sure what we were waiting for, but where other parts of my life felt like they were full of chaos, my relationship with him was equal parts calm and exciting. There was still some hesitation I was holding onto, something in the back of my mind that kept making me ask myself if it was smart to let myself develop feelings for him. As if I had a fucking choice in the matter.

"Things with Javier are doin' well." I suddenly found the vase of dying flowers on the table in front of us very interesting. "We're mostly focusin' on tryin' to get this thing with the Wards over with."

I'd, of course, been keeping Clyde in the loop. He claimed it didn't matter how sad and stressed he was with the situation with his aunt; he needed to know what was going on at home.

He was so quiet in response, I had to look at him to see his reaction. He was giving me a face he'd given me many times before. The same one he'd had when he'd caught me lying about not drinking shine when I was underage, or when I'd denied wanting to go away for school. Just as it had those other times, his expression cracked my chest open, but unlike other times, I didn't fold under the pressure. I stayed silent.

"You know, it's all right to like your husband, little girl." He gave me a small smile. "You don't need to be ashamed of that."

"I know." I closed my eyes briefly.

"Do you?" He refused to let up. "Leadin' ain't easy, Hannah. It sure ain't easy now and it ain't goin' to be easy even when things calm down. I know you love it, and I know how happy our business makes you. But ain't nothin' wrong with wantin' to have somethin' else in your life that makes you feel good. For your mama, it was you girls. Joy always said the work of raisin' you and Nicole was what kept her on the ground. For you, maybe it's Javier, or maybe it ain't. But, if it is, you don't need to feel any kind of way about it."

"It's only been a few weeks, Clyde." I ran my fingers

through the hair at the back of my head. "I think it's a little too soon to talk about the man bein' my peace or whatever."

"I saw you when you walked in here." He smirked. "Skin all glowin', eyes all bright. Seems to me he's already makin' you happy."

"Jesus, Clyde." My eyes widened at the suggestive nature of his words. It was the first time he'd ever said anything like that to me before.

He laughed at my scandalized face. "Ain't nothin' to be ashamed of, Hannah. I don't mean to put your business on front street or nothin', I'm just tellin' you not to be afraid to chase happiness wherever you can find it. I don't care if it comes from Benicio Meza's boy or sellin' them little scarves and hats you always makin'. Whatever it is, find it and hold on to it before you get too caught up to realize you deserve somethin' good." He pressed a warm kiss to my forehead.

I didn't have anything to say back to him. I may not have wanted to agree with him, verbally, but I knew he had a point. Preserving my family's business and way of life was my passion. It was the only career I'd ever wanted to have, the only path I'd ever truly considered for myself. It would be my constant for as long as I could keep it that way.

But it wasn't the only thing I wanted.

Even before meeting Javier, I'd dreamed about starting a small family of my own. Having kids to pass something down to, having a partner to come home to at the end of the day. Both were things I wanted in conjunction with one another.

Mama had been different. She'd married my father because marriage was something everyone else did, but I never got the feeling she cared much about romantic entangle-ments. She'd said many times they only distracted her from the two things she really cared about, the business and her kids. Joy Hawkins cared about being in love about as much as she cared about what other people thought of her, which was not at all.

Since she died, I'd been trying my damndest to be like her. I'd made my own decisions, but not without thinking of what she would have thought about them first—from the way she spoke to people to the phrases she'd used and the life rules she'd followed. I'd considered her the perfect leader and I wanted to be like her. The only issue was that I wasn't like her, not in many crucial ways. We shared the same vision for our family's future, sure, but when it came to our lives, we were very different.

I hadn't noticed how much my poor imitation of my mother in my work had bled over into my personal life. I wasn't saying I would have been starry-eyed and completely gone over Javier had we gotten together when Mama was still alive. Hell, the history between our families meant it might have taken a miracle for me to even give him a chance. I would have been less hesitant, though, especially after he'd shown me what a good man he was, and how open and honest and eager he was to make us work.

In the end, I wanted to be happy. Now, I realized I wanted to seek that happiness with Javier. The thought of having him tuck himself in close to me in bed every night gave me a bright feeling in my chest. Knowing I had the chance to spend my evenings cooking dinner with him in our kitchen made my head spin. I wasn't even going to let myself get into thoughts of possible kids yet, but Javier Meza was starting to appear pretty heavily whenever I pictured my future. All that was left was to get out of my damn head and stop myself from shutting those thoughts down whenever they came up. I needed to chill the fuck out and do what Clyde had suggested, let myself chase my own happiness. I just hoped like hell Javier was actually as open to the idea as he seemed to be.

I stayed with Clyde for a few hours, sitting in the hospital room with him even after his Aunt Clara woke up. Even with her obvious lethargy and pain, the woman was hilarious and kind and I could tell Clyde regretted not having known her better before the end of her life. I wrote Clyde a check from my personal account, making him promise me to spend it on anything he or his aunt needed to feel more comfortable. I also requested he take his time and not rush home while he still had unfinished business in Louisville.

I left the hospital around three-thirty. Javier's best friend, Adrian, was supposed to be having dinner at the house, so I wanted to get home before eight. But before I officially got on the road home, I made a quick stop.

I'd heard about a new ice cream shop in the city that was supposed to have the best non-dairy ice cream for miles. The grocery store in Harlan did what most of us needed it to do. It kept us from being a food desert with plenty of fresh produce and meat, but it didn't have much in the way of anything fancy. They barely had more than plain old chocolate and vanilla ice cream, let alone stuff safe for people with lactose intolerance.

We hadn't talked about the treat much, so I didn't know what flavors Javier would have preferred, so I got a few—one chocolate because I figured everyone loved it, cookies and cream because I knew he enjoyed Oreos, and one with bourbon flavoring and pretzel chunks because I thought it'd be cute and on the nose. Each one of them was free of dairy and safe for him to eat without destroying his stomach.

Once they realized I'd be driving almost four hours with the pints, the shop even packaged them for me the way they did when they were overnight shipping their wares across the country.

I decided to keep the still in the truck bed until the next morning, too eager to get home to Javier to consider stopping. I smiled when I didn't see another car save for mine and Javier's outside the house. I wanted a little while alone with him before Adrian got there.

I could hear him working in the kitchen as soon as I opened the door.

"That you, Hannah?" he called out over the low music he was playing.

I didn't answer until I was standing in the kitchen door-way. "It's me."

He turned to look at me, his handsome face making me falter just a little bit. "How was it?"

"It was fine. The drive was smooth, gettin' the still was smooth, Clyde was...well, not exactly smooth but he's hangin' in there." I walked over to him and pressed my lips to his, this time not even bothering to try to stamp down the tingly feeling in my belly.

"That's good to hear." He was shredding up some pork with his hands so he didn't reach out to touch me, but he did trail a few kisses along the underside of my jaw. "You eat all the snacks I sent you with?"

"Yes daddy, damn!" I rolled my eyes playfully.

He didn't even bother to hide the triumphant grin on his face. Then, his eyes drifted back to the box I held underneath my right arm. "You bring me a gift?"

"Yes, actually." I sat the box down on the table and grabbed a knife out of the utensil drawer before cutting the security tape open and pulling out a pint. "I bought you some ice cream."

His eyes ran across the label, and when he looked back at me, I couldn't quite decipher the look on his face. The next thing I knew, he was abandoning the pork and grabbing me up close to him.

"You bought me ice cream," he said softly, his lips brushing the shell of my ear.

"Dairy-free…"

"You're just tryin' to make me spend the rest of my life showin' you appreciation for bein' so damn good to me, ain't you?" His tongue touched my earlobe first before his lips captured it. I shivered, instantly thankful I hadn't worn any earrings that day.

"I like what happens when you're thankful for me." I ran my hands up his strong back, my fingers digging lightly into the muscles in his shoulders.

"I'm always thankful for you, wife." His breath in my ear made my teeth shatter and my thighs clench together.

"And I—"

The doorbell rang twice and a series of hard knocks sounded on the front door. Javier cursed and pulled away, giving me another peck before he went to get the door.

He'd prepared BBQ pulled pork sandwiches and freshly cut shoestring fries for dinner. He, Adrian, and I sat at the dining room table as we ate. Adrian Padilla Ruiz was nice, respectful, and quiet, even more so than Javier. I learned he was originally from Tennessee and had moved to Cumberland with his mother as a kid. He and Javier met when his mother started working as a runner for the Mezas. He was an Algebra professor at Eastern Kentucky University, and he and Javier took turns traveling back and forth every few weeks to see each other.

I loved watching them interact. It was easy to see how comfortable they were with each other; their conversation and laughter flowed even after spending so much time apart. We talked about their childhood, Adrian's job, and even about the reason we didn't tend to concern ourselves with the laws surrounding moonshining changing. It wasn't until Javier came back with a few bowls and a pint of his brand-new chocolate ice cream that the conversation turned to our relationship.

"Y'all look happy." Adrian's eyes moved back and forth between Javier and me. "All things considered."

It was the second time in a day I'd heard someone mention I looked happy as a direct result of Javier. I would have been offended had I not known they weren't implying I'd looked unhappy before him.

"The marriage wasn't a total bust," I joked. "You know how good the man cooks, Adrian. The pulled pork alone made it all worth it."

Both men laughed, but Adrian eyed me knowingly. "I'm serious," he said. "My boy's got more life behind the eyes than he's had in years. That's got to be your doin'."

I looked over at Javier. "Is that my doin', Javier?"

He took a spoonful of chocolate ice cream, briefly closing his eyes in pleasure at the taste. "I wasn't plannin' to get all sappy tonight."

"For once," I joked.

"But yeah, actually. Hannah's had a big influence on gettin' me out of my own head, on makin' me happy these last few weeks." He had his eyes on me the entire time he spoke.

I ducked my head as my cheeks got hot. I didn't know what to say, so I reached across the table and took his free hand.

"So, does that mean y'all are goin' to stay together when this thing with the Wards is over?" Adrian was determined to dig deeper.

I looked at Javier again. His brown eyes were burning, searching mine for answers. Earlier in the hospital, I'd admitted to myself I needed to take a leap of faith, to chase my own happiness. As open as he was, it was obvious Javier wanted an answer from me before he gave his own. It was fair; I'd been much more closed mouthed than him when it came to my feelings. But fuck if it wasn't hard as hell to form the words.

"I don't think either of us is in a rush to get rid of each other," I said.

It wasn't everything, it was a little tepid, and it certainly wasn't an admission of love. But from the way Javier's fingers tightened in mine and the smile that spread across his face, I knew it was enough for him.

# CHAPTER 17

JAVIER

A few days turned into a week, which became two, then four. The day after Adrian came by the house for dinner, Pop and Hannah held a meeting at my parents' house. Hannah had changed my father's mind about waiting a few days for us to start questioning the brothers. Instead, she suggested we wait longer, a lot longer—at least a month—before we approached them again. She wanted them haggard and desperate to be released. In the meantime, we would keep them sufficiently fed and relatively clean and have two sets of eyes on them at all times.

According to her and Pop, the men watching them had reported the two had already started breaking a week in. By week four, the Ward brothers would have given them the numbers to their bank accounts, their fancy cars, and their father's deepest secrets had they asked.

It was concerning that their father hadn't come snooping around in our neck of the woods looking for them. We'd kept Sam and Cameron on their house in the weeks following the kidnapping. A few men had come by a couple of days after, using a key to let themselves in the front door. The boys said they'd rooted around the house for about an hour and then left. After that, the property hadn't been visited by anyone, not even the gardener or cleaning lady who normally showed up every Wednesday. None of us were stupid. We knew the lack of uproar probably meant Barrett Ward was lying in wait somewhere in the grass.

We made sure to stay vigilant, had guys watching the Hawkins' house and my parents' house at all times. We made sure the kitchen and still houses on Black Mountain were heavily watched. It was frustrating and maddening, and I had no idea how we were surviving it. I asked Hannah how she found it so easy to be patient when she knew there was so much more she could be doing to actively curb the problem. She'd said it wasn't easy, not at all, but she was confident her plan would work. So confident, she was willing to bet the upper hand we'd gained on it.

So, we waited. Hannah and I became more anxious as more days passed. However, we used it to our advantage. Where we worked on a hands-off policy when it came to the Ward brothers, she and I spent as much time together as possible. She worked during the day, running errands, checking in on her shine stock, making sure the ledgers looked good. I'd finally rejoined my stillers, making moonshine on Black Mountain in the evenings. We made time for each other in the morning when I was getting home. I'd climb into bed with her for a couple of hours until she woke up.

She even started making sure to come home late in the

afternoon so we could have dinner together every evening. We developed a routine, one I didn't seem to have any trouble settling into. The more I got to know her, the more I dreaded being away from her.

Hannah was in the shower when I left for my hour-long drive to Black Mountain. I'd taken advantage of being one of the bosses to arrive a little later than everyone else, though there was still plenty of light to the sky by the time I reached the small peak we worked on. The mountain really was a beautiful sight. Under the thick brush of trees and rough terrain, it was easy to feel invincible and invisible from the world outside. I understood why the Hawkins were so protective of their space.

I got no chance to enjoy the beauty of it that night. As soon as I neared the stilling house, I heard voices shouting, completely unintelligible and aggressive. I broke into a run, unsurprised when I came across two men, one of mine and one of Hannah's, pushing and shoving at each other. I adjusted the wide brim of my hat and ran over to them.

"What the hell is goin' on here?" I didn't like raising my voice in anger, and definitely not at my people, but I was in no mood to break up a fight.

"This fuckin' asshole put his hands on me for no reason," yelled Noah, one of my youngest and newest stillers.

"No reason?" I didn't know the other man's name but he looked furious. "You were handlin' that brand new still like you'd never seen one in your life." The man turned to me. "If this is how y'all took care of your equipment down there, maybe it was a blessin' in disguise the Wards shut y'all down."

Noah pushed the man again, forcing him back by his shoulders only for the other man to capture him in a headlock.

"Hey, hey!" I yelled even louder, physically forcing them apart as I stood between them with my hands on their chests. "Stand the fuck down. Do y'all know how much shit we got goin' on right now?"

I could feel their chests expand and collapse at rapid rates. Then, they both nodded.

"You do, then?" I looked back and forth. "And here you are, still behavin' like a couple of plum fools."

"It ain't foolish to take care of what's ours, Meza." Hannah's man had his jaw clenched so tight, I was afraid he'd crack a tooth.

"You ain't protectin' shit," Noah argued. "I wasn't goin' to break that damn thing, I was just tryin' to figure out how to work it."

"All right, all right, both of y'all just calm the hell down." I didn't take my hands off of their chests, but I lowered my voice. "Noah, I know these stills work differently than ours do, but that doesn't give you free rein to be rough with them. Remember, this shit ain't ours so we need to be more careful with it."

I could tell he was still worked up, but he nodded his agreement anyway.

I turned to the other man. "Uh—"

"Nathaniel," he said gruffly.

"Right. Nathaniel. I know this is frustratin' for you, havin' us here and all, but you got to understand that we're tryin'. We're tryin' to stay out of your way and get used to the setup you have here." I sighed. "I know Noah was rough with your shit, but I also know he didn't mean it. There ain't no reason for y'all to be fightin' like two little boys over it. The next time I see you puttin' hands on one of my guys over some petty shit like this, you're going to have me to contend with."

"Man get the fuck off me." Nathaniel shook my hand off his chest and took a step back. "I don't have no interest in workin' with you motherfuckers. Just make sure your boy over here don't fuck up my still and stays the out of my goddamn way and there won't be no more problems."

He didn't leave any room for argument as he walked off with his shoulders drawn tight.

I turned back to Noah. "Go on and get back to work. I'll be in there in a minute to make sure you know how to work the still."

I hadn't had a cigarette since my early twenties, but I craved one of the damn things after that. Working with the Hawkins had been relatively simple; the families tended to tolerate each other. Normally, it was easy seeing as we only crossed paths briefly, but there were times like the one I'd just experienced when things boiled over. We'd had a few fights in the month we'd been working together and while we'd gotten through without any bloodshed, each and every one made me wonder if the Hawkins and Mezas were going to rip each other apart before the Wards even got the chance.

Hannah was up when I got home in the morning. I was

surprised, mostly because she tended to sleep in on Saturdays unless she had something to do. I caught her at the kitchen table, clad in one of my T-shirts and a pair of shorts. She had her hair down, swishing around her shoulders. It was a little messy, the way it was whenever she used her silk pillowcase instead of wrapping it. I knew she was still half asleep when she didn't look up to see me standing in the doorway.

"Is that my ice cream?" I chuckled as I looked down into the bowl she was eating out of.

Hannah jumped a bit at the sound of my voice before blinking up at me. "Jesus." She pressed her hand over her heart. "I figured I'd make you breakfast when you got home this mornin', but you were takin' so long I needed a snack."

"Since when is ice cream at eight in the mornin' a snack?"

"Since it was the only thing that sounded good to me." She smiled.

"I appreciate it, but I grabbed something at the diner on the way in." I winced. "I figured you'd be asleep still."

"Ugh, fine. I guess that just means this has to be my breakfast then."

"Mornin' baby." I chuckled and leaned down to give her a kiss and steal a spoonful of ice cream. "You sleep all right?"

She shrugged. "I missed you in bed with me earlier."

I leaned against the counter a couple feet away from her. "You can keep me in bed all weekend. I ain't got shit to do but be with you for the next two days."

"Damn." She stood up and moved in front of me, her arms going around my waist. "That sounds better than the grits I was goin' to make you for breakfast."

She let out a bark of laughter at the grimace that appeared on my face.

"What? You don't like my grits?" Those brown eyes got all big and round.

"They ain't good, Hannah. You put sugar in them."

"You still eat them, though!"

"I only do it because I love you…" I stopped abruptly and swallowed.

Hannah's eyes got even wider.

That wasn't something I'd ever said to her, not jokingly or otherwise. I'd been avoiding saying the word to myself, in relation to her, even when I knew what I felt was true.

A million things started running through my head as we stood there, silently staring at each other. I thought about our relationship, how much we'd grown in such a short amount of time. I thought about her bringing me dairy-free ice cream knowing I was lactose intolerant, how at home I felt whenever I had her in my arms, and how I couldn't stop thinking about filling her grandmother's house with a bunch of Meza-Hawkins babies.

*Shit.*

Of course, I loved her. She'd given me no goddamn choice but to love her.

"I love you," I repeated, my eyes unflinching as they stared her down.

Hannah's breaths were heavy. A look crossed her face that, for a minute, looked like distress. I wanted to ask her what she was thinking about, beg her to reply to my statement even if it was only to say she didn't feel the same. Whether she raised me up or cut me down, I needed something from her, some answer that helped the tightening coil in my stomach release.

"I love you too," she said after a while, making my head spin. "God fuckin' help me, but I do."

"I want to have a life with you," I continued, wanting to make my intentions plain to her. "I want it all, family, kids, you as my wife. Just thinkin' about it makes me too damn happy for words."

Instead of replying to me, she unraveled her arms and made her way out of the kitchen. "Wait right there and don't move," she said, leaving me staring behind her, dumbstruck.

A couple of minutes later, I heard her heavy footsteps thundering down the stairs. When she came back into the kitchen, she was holding a few pieces of paper. "I printed these off after we came back from Nashville."

They were annulment papers, the preliminary paperwork as provided by the state of Kentucky on their website according to the message at the bottom. They hadn't been filled out, but the sight of them made me nauseous.

Then, I watched as she ripped them all straight down the middle, gathered the two sides up, ripped them again, and then once more for good measure. It was a dramatic gesture, but it sent my heart thumping.

"You know I've been talkin' about this thing between us bein' doomed from the start but I," she swallowed, "I don't want to leave you. I want the same things you want."

I had her up and in my arms again, her ass in my hands

and her legs around my waist as I ached to be as close to her as physically possible.

"Remember when you told me you were goin' to make me so happy that night we kissed for the first time?" She rubbed the tip of her nose against mine.

"Of course, I do."

"You do, Javier." Her thighs tightened around me. "You make me the happiest I've been in a long time. Too long."

"I'm not goin' to stop, either. Not ever."

# CHAPTER 18

HANNAH

My head was a rush of thoughts and emotions. I was giddy and terrified and hopeful, and surprised at how aroused I was. Hearing Javier talk about wanting to spend his life with me had my body humming with pleasure.

Kissing him was becoming instinctual. Anytime I felt overwhelmed, the feeling of his lips on mine helped to ground me. This time, it did the exact opposite. Javier was more passionate than he'd ever been. His mouth was rougher, more insistent. Those big hands squeezed my ass tight.

He turned around and sat me on the cleared kitchen counter so he could clutch at the thickness of my hips under my shirt. I could feel his dick against my stomach, hard and thick. He wasn't even trying to press it into me, but it was impossible to deny.

Javier's kisses left my mouth, pressing wetly against the underside of my jaw. When that tongue hit the sensitive skin of my neck, I started panting. My own thighs were quivering, wrapped so firmly around his waist I couldn't even press them together to soothe the ache in my pussy.

I still hadn't had Javier's dick inside me there yet. I'd felt all over it, had it fuck deep in the back of my throat, but we hadn't fucked each other in that way. I hadn't stressed myself out over it, figuring we'd get there when we got there. The man had already given me a world of pleasure—every time that tongue touched my clit or I got to wrap my hand around that thick dick of his, I burned.

Those things weren't to be diminished, but as Javier's mouth laved over one of my hard nipples through my thin T-shirt, the only thing I wanted was for him to fill me, finally.

Javier seemed to want that too, and he didn't even try to be cute or coy when he brought it up.

"I want to fuck you, wife." His voice was gruff, and he left one nipple untouched as he pulled back to look into my eyes. "Right here on this fuckin' counter, where I had your lips for the first time."

"God." I was breathless in my relief.

"You want that too?" His hands were back on my legs, those calloused thumbs digging a little into my outer thighs. "You want me to take you right here?"

"If you don't, I might explode." I had to laugh a little at my own desperation. "I never felt an ache like this before."

"Where do you ache, Hannah?"

I took one of his hands, guiding it away from my leg to the crux of my thighs. I didn't have on any panties, but I was wearing shorts. Even still, I knew he could feel the heat of my cunt through the crotch.

"You ache here?" His fingers trailed up and down my slit through the material. "Why does this sweet pussy ache, wife?"

I didn't think he was expecting an answer, but I gushed one out anyway. "It aches for you," I admitted. "It aches because it hasn't had you yet."

Javier's hands slipped down the waistband of my shorts so he could touch me without a barrier. "I can tell. This pussy is so hot." I sucked in a breath as he slid a finger into me. "So wet."

I was overcome with the need to get my hands on him. I made my way past his belt and into his jeans, pulling his dick free as I worked my hand up and down. I'd watched Javier jerk himself off so I knew what he liked. He hadn't been rushed then, all slow, languid strokes. My husband was a man who liked to savor his pleasure, even when it came at his own hand.

"Seems like you're achin' too," I said against his mouth.

His hips canted forward a bit when I rubbed my thumb over the tip, my thumb pressing a bit into his slit. "That ain't nothin' new." He bit at my bottom lip. "Every time I'm all up on you like this, my dick gets to pulsin'."

We went at each other at an unhurried pace. The longer his fingers fucked me, the wetter I became. Javier's cock got a little redder around the tip the more worked up he got. I couldn't take my eyes off him. My handsome man with his pupils dark and dilated, Javier in a state of pleasure was something I knew I'd never get tired of seeing.

When I felt the pressure in my belly rise, I pulled away

from him, letting go of the grip I had on his dick. "I'm ready," I told him before he could ask me. "I can't wait any longer."

Javier pulled his fingers from my pussy, bringing them up to my mouth to clean off. Everything was so heady, the taste of myself, the scent of us both in the air, the bite of the hard counter beneath my ass. By the time Javier worked our clothes off, I was writhing.

"Go ahead and slide me in you, wife." He had his hands back on my thighs, this time grabbing them from the insides. "Fill yourself up with this dick."

I took him by the base, rubbing the head along my slit to wet him up some. I couldn't resist letting his head stroke my clit a few times. The small amount of relief it gave me wasn't nearly enough, but it made the teeth digging into my bottom lip lighten up. Both of us hissed when I finally guided him into me.

My pussy opened to him easily, his size stretching and filling, dragging against my walls so beautifully it made me want to cry. Javier's mouth was on my left nipple when he started making shallow thrusts into me. The points at the tips of my heavy breasts were hard in his wet mouth, sending shocks through my entire body as the pleasure from both parts of my body combined.

I had my hands on Javier's tight ass, pulling him deeper into me as his thrusts sped up.

"I see why we waited," I panted in his ear. "I might not have been ready for this dick before."

He bit down sharply on my nipple, leaving it alone to ache

and sting as he looked back up at me. "I don't know about that. You seem to be takin' it real well right now."

We both looked down at where we were joined. The sight of his dick, fucking into me, covered and shiny with my cream almost made me agree with him.

"Maybe." I strummed my clit, rubbing it in long, slow circles. "But if I'd had it before, I definitely would have fallen earlier."

"Dick good enough to make you fall in love, huh?" Little beads of sweat had popped up on his forehead.

I could only nod as his strokes became more forceful. My ass moved more on the counter, and I clutched onto him to stay where I was and take what he had to give me.

Javier kept talking, his voice rougher and more breathless than I'd ever heard it. "I get it, though. You're wrapped around me so good. All warm and grippin' me like you don't want me to leave. I'm already in love with this pussy."

"I fuckin' love it when you talk to me like that," I groaned. "That filthy ass mouth."

"You bring it out in me." Javier had my thighs up and in his hands, keeping my legs spread wide so he could fuck me deep. "I just want to tell you how good you feel, how much I want to spend all my days makin' you and this pussy happy and satisfied."

"Just stay with me." I was fucking him back in earnest, moving my hips on his cock as much as I could, given the position. "Just keep fuckin' me like that and I'll be more than satisfied."

He didn't reply again, but I was too wrapped up in pleasure to care. I shook as wave after wave of pleasure took over me. Javier looked at me with hooded eyes as the fingers on my clit moved faster, more pointed and steady, as I chased after my orgasm. His dick dragged against my walls, pushing against my spot over and over again with the help of his rhythmic strokes.

I came silently, my brain stuttering and then going blank as pleasure made my entire body feel like I was wading through a heavy ocean. I didn't register the slight pain in the back of my head as it hit the cabinet behind me, nor did I take stock of my knuckles whitening as I dug my short nails into the planes of Javier's back.

My clit pulsed and my pussy gushed around Javier's thrusting dick. When I opened my eyes again, I saw that his thighs and stomach were wet.

"Shit." He reached down to take the base of his dick in his hand before he pulled out of me. He stroked himself, using what I'd left behind on him to guide the way.

"Come on me," I requested, overcome with the need to have him cover me the same way I'd covered him. "Right here." I stoked my hands over the curls of my mons and my thighs. "Come on my pussy, Javier. Give it to me."

He erupted at my words, his pearly come spilling from him in streams as he gave me exactly what I wanted. I could feel it all over the lips of my pussy, in the creases of my thighs, and on the chubby flesh that made up my lower belly.

I rubbed it in a little as I panted, the feel of it slippery and hot underneath my fingers. I loved how warm it was, how it was evidence of the fact I'd gotten him off so thoroughly.

Javier leaned forward to nuzzle me, his nose rubbing against my cheeks and jaw as his breathing evened out.

"My wife." He whispered it softly into the hollow of my neck. "My Hannah."

I wrapped my arms around him again, gasping softly with the need to be as close to him as physically possible. I would have burrowed into him if I could, but I could already feel the warmth of his insides surrounding me, cloaking me in every ounce of love he had to give. I pressed in deeper, wanting him to feel mine too.

"My husband."

After a long night working and a morning of fucking me in our kitchen, Javier needed rest. I, however, was wide awake and wired.

Instead of trying to fall back asleep or sit around the house waiting for him to wake up, I met Lex at Kenny's. It was an old-school diner in town everyone visited when they didn't feel like traveling somewhere else to eat out. Before my life had become so hectic, Lex and I had breakfast there together every Saturday along with Mama and Nicole. In the past couple of weeks, we'd gotten back to that. In trying to be more like myself and less like my mother, I made a concentrated effort not to isolate myself.

"I heard there was another fight on the mountain last night," Lex commented as she cut into her French toast.

I sighed. Javier had called me after it happened. He'd apparently handled it pretty well, and I wasn't about to dig the knife in any further by confronting Nathaniel about it, but I was definitely frustrated.

"Yeah. Honestly, I don't know that we're even goin' to get those guys to stop tryin' to fuck each other up every chance they get."

"Is there any news about when the Mezas will be able to go back to their own kitchen?"

I picked at the fruit salad in front of me. "I talked to Benicio this week. They only just started gettin' the materials they need to rebuild." I shrugged. "He says their contractor estimated it might be another three months or so before they can move back in."

"Damn." Lex's cheeks dimpled as she grimaced. "You think y'all are goin' to survive 'til then?"

"You are so damn dramatic! I know everybody on both sides will be happy as hell to get back to normal when we can, but they'll deal for now. Either that or they can take their asses on somewhere."

"Hmm." There was a little smirk on her oval-shaped face.

"What?"

"Nothin' just..." Lex leaned back and crossed her arms over her chest. "You sound confident, that's all. More sure of yourself and shit."

"Remember a few months ago when Mama died, and we were at that club in Lexington and you told me I needed to channel my inner bad bitch more often?"

Lex laughed loudly, making people at a few of the surrounding tables look over at us. "Yeah."

"Well, that's what I'm doin'. I'm just usin' it to lead a bunch of moonshiners instead of gettin' lame dudes to buy us drinks." I grinned at her.

"Well, I'm proud of you. You're gettin' good dick, bein' the boss you were meant to b—" She stopped, her face transforming from a smile to a scowl in a second as she looked behind me. "Can we fuckin' help you?"

I turned around, and my eyes landed on a tall man in an expensive suit. I'd never seen him before, but something about him was incredibly familiar. The incredibly straight nose, the cold blue eyes, that blond hair that looked almost unnaturally yellow. All of it combined clicked into place as recognition clouded my brain.

The man must have been Barrett Ward—he couldn't have been anyone else. Judging by the clarity in his eyes, he knew who I was too.

"Hannah Hawkins, I presume." He had that slightly lifted, pretentious cadence all the rich people around us seemed to have.

"Barrett Ward." I said his name, wanting him to know he hadn't caught me completely unawares.

His smile made me uneasy. "You look just like your mother, Hannah."

I almost knocked my chair over when I stood up from the table. I heard Lex's scratch against the floor.

"Don't talk about my mother," I forced out. "You didn't know her."

"Yes, I did." I knew he wasn't lying, immediately, and I felt queasy. "I met with her many times, in this diner, actually."

I wanted to run away—to the bathroom to release the contents of my stomach, back home to curl up under Javier. I wanted to run anywhere that wouldn't make me confront the possibility of my mother having a connection to the Wards.

Barrett's eyes strayed to Lex behind me, staying on her for a few seconds before he looked back at me. "I'd like to speak to you alone, Miss Hawkins."

"For what?" I snapped, my voice brittle.

"You know what." He remained outwardly unaffected.

"Fine." I grabbed my purse from the back of my chair. "Outside. You and that ugly ass suit are freakin' everybody in here out."

"Hannah…" Lex looked at me and I could tell she was ready to follow me.

"I'm fine." I tried to sound as comforting as possible but by the way her face fell, I knew I'd failed. "This is business stuff. I'll take care of it. Just stay here until I get back, okay?"

She yielded, sitting back down in her chair with her fist clenched as I walked outside to the front of the diner with Barrett. I took him towards my car parked in the front of the building towards the end of the parking lot.

"We're not givin' you your sons back until you promise to leave us the hell alone," I told him as soon as we were away from any prying eyes.

It was a hot day, the June sun beating down on the asphalt we stood on. As soon as he started sweating, he pulled a white handkerchief out of his pocket and swiped it across his forehead. My lip curled.

"The boys can wait. I'm here to see if you'd be interested in the same deal I had with your mother."

When Barrett mentioned having met with my mother in

the past, I'd assumed he meant something like that. Actually, having him confirm it was heartbreaking and disgusting. Why would she have done something so dirty? What could she possibly have gained from it? My mother wasn't greedy, not for money or notoriety. She didn't need to be. Not for the first time, I wished she was there with me so that I could question her, rage at her and ask her what the hell she'd been thinking.

"If you're worried about Joy being some kind of villainous betrayer, you needn't." He smirked. "I approached her, not the other way around."

"What did you want from her?"

"I wanted her to help me get rid of the Mezas." He looked past me towards the tree line. "Obviously, she didn't come through on her end before she died, so I followed through on my promise to take her family out along with them. Unfortunately, you deciding to join up with them has made that difficult, especially now that you've taken my idiot sons hostage." He pursed his lips. "But I'm more than willing to offer you the same deal I gave Joy."

His suggestion was rooted in arrogance, so much so it made me let out a chuckle in an otherwise dark moment. "Since when are you in any position to ask anythin' of me? Your sons may be idiots, but they're still yours and we still have them. All we have to do is threaten to end their lives and you'll have no choice but to back off."

"You and I both know you aren't going to kill my boys, Miss Hawkins. We don't even need to play those games."

He was right. It didn't matter how intense things got. I

already knew no one on either side wanted to stoop that low. I wasn't going to admit that to Barrett, though.

"But you know me," he continued. "You know exactly what I'm capable of, what I'm willing to do to get what I want. You can refuse to take my offer if you want, but if you do, I'll make sure hell rains down on that mountain your people hole themselves up on. Whether it be fire like we gave the Mezas or the law. The real law, not these no-good county sheriffs you've been dealing with. Either way, I'll make it my personal mission to make the Hawkins name disappear from this town completely before I move on to the Mezas."

His words were frightening, but I also felt relief at the fact my mother had only agreed to his little plan out of desperation to keep our family alive.

"So, this is what you threatened my mother with? This is what you told her to make her do something so low down and dirty as agree to work with you against the Mezas?"

"Yes." He made another swipe with the handkerchief, this time along his upper lip. "I was actually surprised I had to, though. I'd heard you guys were rivals, but it took threatening her own family to get her to go against a group of people she couldn't even stand."

"That's because we have rules up here." I thought back to the decades of tradition I'd been taught. "The Mezas may be our rivals, but we hate outsiders like you more than we could ever hate them."

"And does this loyalty you have for them mean you're willing to bring your family down?" He raised one of his pale eyebrows.

That, I didn't have an answer to. I wanted to say no, say I'd stand with the Mezas to protect my integrity, but I had an entire family to think about. More than a few people were counting on me to feed their families and to keep our status, in the tumultuous place we called home, as high as possible so we stayed nearly untouchable by the people who didn't want us there.

I knew the Mezas faced the same thing too; they were under the same threat we were. Had they been in my position, would Benicio had gone along with Barrett's plan? Would Javier?

God, Javier. I'd just admitted I loved him hours before. For me to even consider betraying his family while claiming to care for him had me disgusted. Worse than that, even.

The sick feeling in my stomach was back, making it gurgle and seize. I didn't know what the hell to do, and I needed to buy a little bit of time so I didn't have to give him an answer right away.

"Why do you want the Mezas gone so bad anyway?" I questioned. "How are they so different from us that you want them taken out instead?"

I scoffed when he made no move to answer me.

"If you think I'm goin' to agree to fuck up my deal with them for you without knowin' why I'm doin' it, you're out of your damn mind."

"They have something I want." His eyes blazed. "A piece of land Benicio's father bought from mine a long time ago."

The man was filthy rich. What the fuck could a plot of land in Cumberland, Kentucky mean to him?

"What's so special about this land?" I couldn't stop myself from voicing my curiosity. I was positive he was going to reveal he and his family wanted to set up shop in the mountains and start a little moonshine operation of their own, as we'd originally thought—using the fact that the Mezas had been taken out in order to snatch up their clientele. Ours too, if we didn't do what he wanted.

"What's special about it is that it's mine," he spat. "My people helped settle this fuckin' dump and that land belonged to Wards for decades before my drunkard father sold it off."

I felt like a fool in an instant. We'd been wrong all along, so wrong we'd wasted valuable time traveling across state lines to strengthen alliances that had never been in any danger.

I would have been shocked by his reasoning if it wasn't almost laughable cliché. Some rich prick feeling so entitled to something so fucking minuscule, something that wasn't even his, he was willing to start a war to steal it.

"And you haven't just tried to," I raised my shoulders, "buy it back? I'm sure Benicio would have much rather sell it to you than be forced to deal with this bullshit."

"Buy it back?" He sounded disgusted. "It's mine. I won't pay someone to give me what's rightfully mine. I'll just take it."

"Only it *ain't* yours."

Barrett's teeth bared a little as he dragged his tongue over his lips, his annoyance clear on his face. "I want a yes or a no, Miss Hawkins." His tone was soft, but I had no trouble hearing him. "Can we work together or do I need to bring my vast resources out in full force to take both of you out?"

It wasn't something I could mull over in my head. I had no real choice—either agree to do what he asked or be obliterated. What good could I do anybody if both the Mezas and the Hawkins were destroyed? At least one name had to stand at all costs.

"Fine." I swallowed the bile rising in my throat. "You've got your deal."

# CHAPTER 19

JAVIER

I'd gotten to sleep for a few hours before the insistent ringing of my phone woke me up. The last time something like that happened, I'd gotten news that had destroyed me. This time, it was news that made me panic. Hannah's voice had been frantic, her words rushed and slightly unintelligible when she requested I meet her at my parents' house immediately.

I'd dressed hastily, thinking something else had gone wrong on Black Mountain or the Wards had gotten free. When I pulled up in front of my folks' place, Hannah was sitting in her car with the windows rolled up and her head against the steering wheel.

She jumped when I tapped on the window. Her eyes were puffy with unshed tears and her face was masked in something I'd never seen on her before—shame.

I waited for her to open up and step out of the car before I pulled her close to me, my hand cradling the back of hers. She let me hold her for a few moments before she pulled away. I noticed she was being careful not to let her tears fall.

"We need to go in, Javier. There's somethin' y'all need to know."

The scene in my parents' kitchen looked like it had the morning we'd come up with the plan to kidnap the Ward brothers, but it was somehow grimmer, though we didn't know why.

*Yet.*

"Barrett Ward approached me at Kenny's Diner this mornin'." She didn't beat around the bush, and it made all of us sit up straighter. "He tried to make me a deal to work with him to take your family down."

"Hold up, hold up." Pop held a hand up to stop her but Hannah kept going. "He had the same one with my mama before she died, too."

"Hannah…" I was unable to say anything else as I tried to wrap my head around what the hell she was revealing.

"He didn't give either of us a choice, not really." She looked around the table, the look in her eyes begging us to understand where she was coming from, but I wasn't sure we could. "He threatened to destroy my family too, to come at us even harder than they have been."

"What did you say, Hannah?" my mother asked. "Did you agree?"

"I didn't have a choice. I had to."

I stood up from my seat at the island and turned my back to her. Everything from my neck to the tips of my ears heated as the anger rose in me.

"You betrayed us," my father hissed. "After all that talk

about fearin' we were goin' to screw you over, you turned around and did it to us."

I didn't have any words. What was there to say when the woman you loved revealed she'd sold your family out to save her own?

"What does he want with us, Hannah?" Mami was the calmest of us all.

"He wants some land you own." I could tell she was making a concentrated effort to speak slowly and clearly. "He said your daddy bought it from him a long time ago and he wants it back. He ain't interested in payin' for it, though."

"What did he mean when he said he wanted you to take us down?" I made sure to keep my eyes locked on Hannah's.

"He wants me to get my family to beat and threaten your people until they're too tired to fight for you anymore. He wants us to make it so you can't distribute anythin' you have left. Then, when he's got you weak and on your knees, he's goin' to threaten to get the Feds on you if you don't hand him the deed to that land and any others you own in the area."

We were all silent after that. We could try to fight the Hawkins. We had more people than them on our team after all, but I wasn't positive we would win, especially not with tensions so high between our people and the Hawkins possibly having the help of the Wards behind them.

Mami was the first one to speak again. She stood, walked around the island, and placed her hands on the arms Hannah had crossed over her chest. "You said you agreed to take his deal, but here you are telling us about it instead of coming up with a plan of action with your people. Why is that?"

"I told him yes, but only to get him from comin' after me immediately. I don't have any plans of betrayin' y'all, Miss Alma." Hannah looked over at me. "I love your son. I won't go against him, and that means I ain't goin' against his family neither."

My legs propelled me over to her. I knew my face was contorted when Hannah's eyes watered again as she stared up at me.

I pressed my lips against her slightly damp forehead, keeping them there for a few beats longer than necessary just because I wanted to feel her. It wasn't the time or the place to have a heart to heart. That would have to wait for later.

Pop got up to join us. For the second time, he put a hand on her shoulder, all three of us circled around her, endlessly grateful she was giving us a chance.

"I'm not givin' that man shit. My daddy got that land fair and square, and I don't care if this family never does anything' with it. Barrett Ward ain't gettin' it, especially not after everything he's done. Well, we've spent plenty of time comin' up with plans to get these pricks out of here, so what's a little more?" my father asked. "We just need to make sure this one really works, makes the Wards scared enough to stay away for good."

———

There was a chill on Black Mountain the next morning. We were well into June, and while the sun was still on its way up, there was no reason I should have regretted not bringing a windbreaker along with me. I'd checked the forecast that morning and saw it was supposed to be clear skies all day, but I could still smell rain in the air.

We hadn't had long to come up with a plan—only hours to pull something together and relay it to our people. We couldn't risk waiting any longer than a day and letting Barrett Ward catch wind to the fact Hannah didn't plan on making good on the deal they'd made.

For the first time in a long time, both the Hawkins and the Mezas were calling all hands on deck. We'd gathered up all our runners and stillers and everyone who existed anyplace in between. Hannah had even called up Clyde, regretfully pulling him away from his sick aunt because she knew he would have been furious had she not. The man had driven in from Louisville in the middle of the night, looking haggard and scarily alert at the same time.

By sunlight, the stretch of Black Mountain we worked on was crawling with people. They'd been instructed to leave their cars someplace near the bottom and hike to the peak so they didn't draw unnecessary attention when Barrett showed up.

I watched the people around me as I herded one of the Ward brothers through the crowd. Everyone seemed to have a purpose. The crowd was full of mixed faces from both families, just as steeled and determined as their leaders were.

"Right here?" Cameron asked from beside me, forcing the other brother in front of him to stop as we came up to a couple of large trees that sat in front of the still houses.

"Yep." I turned Carver around and pushed his back against the bark. "Right here."

They were both in bad shape. They weren't malnourished or even half-dead, but they had very little fight left in them. Pop had made sure none of the men watching them did anything to cause them physical pain while they were locked in our barn, but I could see it had taken a toll on them. Carver barely struggled as I tied him to the tree, making sure the rope was just tight enough to keep him secure but not damage him.

"You stay here with them," I instructed Cameron, watching as he did the same to Avery. "I'll send Sam up this way soon as I see him. All you have to do is stay here until somebody comes to get you. Just don't let them get away."

He adjusted the baseball cap on his head back a bit so I could see his face better. "You got it," he assured me.

When I made it the half-mile back down the mountain to where we normally parked our cars, Hannah was there with her sister and my mother. Both Nicole and Mami had rifles in their hands. I recognized my mother's as the one she and Pop kept locked up in his office at the house.

"I hope you don't have to actually use these," she told them. "But if you do, just make sure you aim somewhere where you'll wound but not kill. The last thing we need is to have to clean up dead bodies once this is all over."

I put my hand on her lower back, letting her know I was there.

"We're goin' to put y'all somewhere in the middle." Hannah pointed over to a thicket of trees where the brush of leaves made it easy to hide. "That way, we'll only need you if Plan A fails."

She didn't turn to me until Mami and Nicole had walked towards their designated spot.

"What's up?" she asked.

"You ready for this?" I couldn't tell how she was feeling from the look on her face, but I could feel the adrenaline pulsing through her, making her skin vibrate.

"I'm ready for this to be over with. I want us to have our peace again. If we don't get it today, I'm scared we'll never have it again."

"We're goin' to win, Hannah." I couldn't let myself believe anything less because I had no idea what any of us would do if we didn't. "Then we're goin' to do that thing we discussed and make each other happy."

She smiled up at me, a genuine one that made me miss the sunshine a little less.

Her phone dinged in her hand, and her smile disappeared as soon as she read the message. Even in the tense moment, I maintained my shock that the cell reception on the mountain was halfway decent.

"Lex says he's on his way up," she said loud enough for anyone standing around us to hear. "There are a couple of cars trailin' behind him, SUVs she said. He brought people with him."

"I guess that means it's straight to Plan B then." My father walked up with Clyde at his side.

"We should have known," Clyde remarked. "You can't put any kind of trust in somebody like that."

"Well, it's a good thing we didn't then, huh?" Hannah turned to me. "Go on and get everybody ready up ahead. We'll lead them to you."

Clyde handed his rifle over to my father and stood at Hannah's side.

"You sure about goin' into this without a rifle?" I asked. I knew her mother had taught her to shoot, which was why I was surprised when she'd revealed she wasn't goin' to have one in hand when she met with Barrett.

"I'll get one when I need one." Her tone was rushed. "I'll be fine until then. Now go!"

Pop and I did as she said, but the clench in my chest made it hard for my legs to move as I looked back to see her and Clyde standing there alone, completely weaponless and more vulnerable than I could stand.

# CHAPTER 20

HANNAH

They filed out of the SUVs in a way that was almost too uniform. Aside from Barrett himself, each of the fourteen men he came with was large with big, muscular arms and legs like tree trunks. They had faces so blank I wondered if Barrett had found them in some kind of super-soldier factory somewhere. Only five of them had guns, but I assumed the others were well prepared to use their fists.

"This wasn't the plan, Barrett," I said to him from across the small makeshift parking lot.

"I never go into a dangerous situation without adequate protection, Miss Hawkins." His eyes roamed over Clyde. Then he looked around at the nature behind me. "I guess all of us aren't so smart. When your mother had me meet her up here, she didn't bring anyone with her either. That naivete must run in the family."

I saw Clyde stiffen, but I wasn't ready to play my hand yet.

I flashed Barrett a fake little smile. "I suspect I invited you up here for a different reason than my mama did." I walked a closer to him, wanting to be able to clearly see the look on his face. "I wanted to tell you I've changed my mind, that I have no intention of goin' against the Mezas."

Barrett rolled his eyes, his face going from fake nice to a sneer. The fury rolled off him in waves, but I wasn't afraid of him. I didn't have the luxury of being scared. I had to believe our people would pull off what we had planned because if I didn't, we were all as good as dead.

"I'm not going to beg you, Hannah." He spoke through clenched teeth. "I've already made my offer to your family twice, and I don't plan on making it again."

"I wouldn't take it even if you did." I clasped my hands behind my back to keep from throwing a punch at his infuriating face.

"Well that settles it then." He turned to his men, signaling for the five that had them to raise their guns.

I was now staring down the barrels of five rifles. I was afraid, but it wasn't nearly enough to get me to back down.

"I have no problems going through the Hawkins to get to the Mezas." He laughed. "And I have even less of a problem starting with you."

"I'm sure you ain't, Mr. Ward, but I don't think you're goin' to get much of a chance to do either of those things."

I whistled low and loud, watching with a smile as they stepped into the light. They came from behind trees and bushes, all pointing rifles towards Barrett Ward and his men. I looked up to see a few people leaning through the greenery at the top of a few of the trees, and then back to face the Ward patriarch. Both Hawkins and Mezas had guns pressed into the intruders' backs.

"You want to follow me?" I asked Barrett, not bothering to wait for an answer before I started walking.

I trekked the trail slower than I normally would have, enjoying the sound of Barrett and his men panting in fear and lethargy as the rough mountain terrain exhausted them.

I could see the larger group of people the second the trees cleared. Their formation wasn't tight or uniform, but they took up plenty of space. Guns in hand, they stood just far apart to make sure no one could move between them if the men tried to run. There were more than fifty people gathered around my still houses, but Barrett Ward's eyes were locked on his boys tied to twin trees in the center of it all.

I led them over to Javier and Benicio who were standing right in front of the trees. The looks on their faces were the kind of relaxed that existed when you were confident you were about to win something big.

"This is Benicio Meza," I introduced. "The man you wanted me to betray." I gestured to the man next to him. "This is his son, Javier. My husband." I turned around and located Alma who was standing next to Nicole, still holding guns to the backs of two of the Ward men. "That's his wife, Alma." I knew I was being dramatic, but I spread my arms wide. "And these are his people. All of them. And they're my people too and you didn't bring nearly enough protection to get rid of all of us."

Ward didn't look at me, keeping his eyes on his sons who'd started struggling as soon as they saw their father.

"Tim," he called out, calm.

"Yes, boss?" the man standing in front of my sister called back.

"Go untie my boys."

Nicole looked at me, an unspoken question in her eyes. I nodded, allowing the man to walk forward until he got to the tree Carver Ward was tied to.

"Sam," Javier called out before the man got the chance to figure out where the rope ended.

Sam stepped out from behind the tree and sent the butt of his rifle into Tim's head hard enough that we all heard the thump. The other man slumped to the ground, sufficiently knocked the hell out.

We all looked over at Barrett. His face and neck were steaming red.

"You'll get them back when you get the fuck out of dodge," Javier called from across the way.

Barrett curled his lip up. He looked at the man next to him. One of the Meza boys still had a gun pressed into the man's back, but he was young and even I could see he was terrified.

"Ray," was all Barrett said before the shot went off.

It went faster than anyone could follow, but when Sam screamed and fell to the ground clutching his side, I knew we wouldn't be leaving the mountain without shedding more blood.

Chaos erupted as a result. Cameron stepped out from behind the other tree and ran to Sam, clutching him as the man yelped in pain.

Cameron raised Sam's shirt up, looking at the wound and then looking back at me. "I think it just grazed him," he called out.

The sigh of relief I let out was audible.

"Take him to the kitchens," I called above the yelling voices. "Get him out of here."

Those who'd been holding guns to the backs of Barrett's men had been shocked out of their upper hand. The ones without reacted quickly, turning my people into targets in a second. I heard both my sister and Alma scream in frustration as they were overpowered to the floor by the men they'd had at gunpoint.

Benicio moved towards his wife faster than I'd ever seen him move, sending a brutal right hook to the man who'd pushed her on the ground before the one who'd pushed my sister held a knife to his neck.

I listened as Javier yelled, telling our people to calm down as he helped Cameron get a good enough hold on Sam to carry him through the woods.

A crack of thunder drew my attention upwards. Clouds opened up through the trees, all of us pausing as a strike of lightning hit and fat droplets of rain pelted down. This was no summer shower, but a storm. One that made the ground underneath us soggy and wet almost immediately.

I took advantage of the distraction to run to where the brothers were tied. Reaching into my back pocket, I pulled out a jackknife, sawing at the ropes until Carver was free. Instead of running to his father, he fell to his knees in the dirt, gasping for air.

I pulled him up by his collar, the nearly dead weight making my joints ache. "Run," I said low in his ear. "Run into the woods or I'll shoot your brother right here in front of you."

Someone stronger would have called my bluff, would have forced me to my knees in defeat. But Carver Ward wasn't strong. He was as downtrodden as I'd ever seen a person as he ran right past his father and into the trees beyond.

I looked over to see Barrett Ward loading a shotgun of his own. I made quick work of the ropes around Avery before sending him off.

"Go after your boys, Barrett," I called as he held his gun up towards me. "Get there before mine do."

I gave a nod to the men along the tree-line which sent them running into the woods. Barrett looked back and forth between me and the heavily wooded area, a snarl leaving his lips when he finally motioned for his men to go in behind them.

I waited until I was sure they were well into the woods to speak. "Go after them," I told the people standing around. "You know this mountain better than they ever could. The rain will make it hard for them to see, but it'll give you the upper hand. Track their footsteps in the mud. Corner them one by one, use force if you have to, hurt them if you have to, but bring them back to me." I turned to Miss Alma and Nicole. "Y'all go back to the kitchen and get Sam to the hospital. Tell them whatever you have to, but don't mention what's goin' on up here."

They dispersed, creeping silently into the brush. Javier stayed by my side along with Benicio.

"I need you two with me," I told them. "Barrett ain't goin' to be alone out there no matter what happens. I don't know what it's goin' to take to get him down, but I know I ain't goin' to be able to do it by myself."

"I'm with you always," Javier said. Benicio backed up the sentiment with a nod.

The heavy rainfall was the only thing keeping the sound of our boots squishing in the mud from alerting people to our presence. Javier and Benicio let me lead, guns raised as they took up my flank on both sides. Both men could find their way around a mountain, even if they didn't specifically know this one well. They knew how to read a compass, how to track where the light streamed in through the trees, and even how to tell when the ground dipped or sloped to let you know which direction you were hiking.

I knew the woods better. We'd played in them as kids whenever Mama would drag us up the mountain on days when she had business to handle. I recognized the smaller fir trees, ones that had only started growing after they'd stopped mining the mountain for coal. I saw the large stone where I'd had my first kiss with Trey Harris, the son of a long-dead stiller. I probably could have trekked through it with my eyes closed and still found my way out of it without getting hurt.

Ward and his men made it incredibly easy, though. I was no expert tracker, but the footsteps along the path ahead of us were another guiding light.

We stopped briefly when we heard a yell in the distance.

The trees rustled against of an obvious struggle, and then it was quiet again. Blood rushed to my ears. I wasn't sure who'd won the fight that had obviously taken place, but I hoped like hell it was one of ours.

It became obvious the people behind the three sets of footprints we were following had no clue where they were going. They zig-zagged, going back and forth as if they couldn't tell which way to go. I leaned down, making out toeprints.

"Neither of the brothers was wearing shoes, right?" I asked Javier and Benicio.

The elder of the two shook his head.

"It's them then." I smiled up at Javier and Benicio. "At least one, but I'm willin' to bet both."

"Their daddy is probably with them then." Benicio looked around. "We're on the right path."

We followed the muddy prints until we came to a clearing, a grassy knoll the size of a medium-sized bedroom surrounded by thick fir trees. All three Barrett men had gathered in the middle. Carver was on the ground, his face contorted as he clutched at his ankle. The rain was pelting down fast, and while I was soaked from the hat I had on to my socks, I smiled at our luck.

We closed in on them before they knew what was happening. Avery raised his hands, fell to his knees next to his brother. Barrett wasn't willing to give up so easily. He raised and cocked his rifle, pointing it straight at me for the second time that day.

Javier grunted and cocked the gun, letting off two shots of his own right next to Barrett's feet.

"We win," I yelled over at the man. "Put that shit down."

Barrett looked over at his boys, his chest rising and falling, hard. The fight had completely left them.

He threw his gun down on the ground towards me, and I picked it up, holding a rifle in my hands for the first time all morning. He didn't drop to his knees, though he allowed Javier to place a ziptie around his wrists and lead him forward. Benicio and I didn't bother with Carver and Avery. They followed without fuss.

The rain was dying down by the time we made it back to the stilling houses. All but one of Barrett's men were on their knees. The one who wasn't was lying on the ground with Donna's foot pressed into his back. It was obvious they'd put up a hell of a fight; for every bruise or scratch or black eye I saw on one of them, my people had two more. Even with the advantage of our numbers, it had still proved difficult for us.

For a moment, I regretted having to turn my people into soldiers. By and large, the Mezas and the Hawkins were peaceful. We wanted to make our moonshine and be left the hell alone. What the Wards had brought out in us, forced us to do and endure, made me furious.

We forced the three Ward men to the ground. Barrett's jaw was hard and defiant as he stared up at me.

"This is over, Barrett." I looked around. "You brought your little army up on my mountain hopin' to start a war, and I gave you what you wanted. Now that you've lost, it's time to run on home."

"I want what's mine," he said, simply.

"Our land doesn't belong to you," Benicio said from his

place next to me. "Hell, it never belonged to you. You ain't gettin' it. I'll put that shit on my dyin' breath if I have to."

"Hear that?" I smiled at him. "Mr. Meza sounds like he's ready to fight you until the very end if he has to. Which means we'll be fightin' too and we've already shown you that you can't win this fight."

Barrett brought the arms that had been tied in front of him up, the ziptie around his wrists splitting open as he slammed his arms down against his hip. Then, he rushed towards me, his face puffy and red with rage.

I cocked the rifle, closed one eye, and aimed, letting a shot off into his shoulder and sending him rearing back on the ground, yelling. Carver and Avery ran to him, crying and yelling and whimpering as their father writhed.

Javier moved in close behind me as I walked up to where Barrett was lying. I was finished playing games with him, through chasing him through the woods and trying to reason with him. I wanted this over and done with.

I pressed the barrel of his own gun deep into his skull. "I'm not my mama, Barrett Ward."

He whimpered.

I raised my foot and pressed it into his shoulder. "She wasn't ready to kill for our family. I guess you hadn't pushed her far enough yet. But this is where you've taken me. Whether it's today, two months from now when you decide to come slitherin' back, or years from now when you think we've forgotten about all this. I'm ready to put a bullet in your head to protect what's mine. It's up to you to decide when and if I'm goin' to have to take it there."

"Bitch!" He called out through gritted teeth.

"I'm a bitch who's this close to signin' your death warrant, that's for damn sure."

He twitched.

I dug both my foot and the gun deeper. "I want an answer, Barrett! Now!"

"Fine," he yelled. "Fine, you hicks can have that piece of shit land. Fine! Just let me go. Let me go to the hospital."

I pulled back but kept the gun raised and asked Javier and Benicio to pull him up.

"Donna?" I called out, keeping an eye on the three Ward men, ones we'd feared so much in the past few months who'd been rendered to dust at the hands of my family. Both my families.

"Yes, Miss Hannah?"

"Lead these boys off of my damn mountain and trail them to make sure they get where they're going." I smiled at her. "Don't let them stop at any of the local hospitals, either. Make them wait until they get home to see if that wound has already started festerin' or not."

# CHAPTER 21

HANNAH

I was exhausted by the time Javier and I made it back home. I was freezing cold, the rainwater that had soaked through my clothes finally catching up to me. My legs ached from the prolonged hiking and my throat hurt from yelling too much. I'd given everyone the next few days off. The fear they'd experienced, the work they'd put in to keep us safe...all of them deserved a little while to rest up before it was time to get back to work.

Javier and I showered together, our touches loving but not sensual as we helped each other get clean and warm. We were meeting up with his parents later that night, but before that, I needed to talk to him, needed to make sure he was all right. That *we* were all right.

I sat close to him on the couch, my bare feet tucked under his warm thighs and my hair pulled up into a deep conditioning cap. Javier sipped a glass of warmed white whiskey, his eyes on me.

"How do you feel?" I was the first one to speak up. "You all right?"

He shrugged. "I'm kind of pissed I never got the chance to beat the shit out of one of those Ward brothers but yeah, I'm doin' fine." He coughed into his fist a couple times.

"And seein' me up there with that gun to Barrett's head, that didn't make you…" I shrugged. "That didn't freak you out or make you think twice about bein' with me?"

Javier looked at me like I'd grown two heads. "Hannah, what else was there for you to do? I ain't goin' to say I enjoyed seein' you in so much danger, but I thought you handled it beautifully. You did what needed to be done. What a leader would have done."

"I think so too," I said, truthfully. "And I did it all without havin' to kill anybody."

We both laughed at that.

My husband took my feet from underneath his thigh and placed them in his lap. His insistent fingers dug into the sole of the right one first, digging and rubbing, his hands warm and causing me to groan.

"How are you feelin' about what you learned about your mama?" His voice was quiet, his tone concerned.

"I don't even know. I don't know if it's worth feelin' anything strong about. She's gone. And it ain't like I can confront her about it." I rubbed a hand over my forehead.

He could tell I wasn't quite finished. "But?"

"I just don't fully understand it," I said. "I don't understand why she didn't think to try to fight off the Wards. Why she didn't tell anybody about Barrett approaching her, not even Clyde. I don't understand any of the decisions she made surrounding that, and it frustrates me I never will."

"Why does it frustrate you so much?" Javier used his thumbs to massage the bottom of my foot.

"Because it was fuckin' stupid!" I growled. "What she did was stupid and reckless. It was nothin' like wh—"

"—what you would have done?" He continued for me when I cut myself off. "Your mama wasn't perfect, Hannah. Not in any part of her life, not even as a leader." He sounded sympathetic, like he was breaking a piece of devastating news to me. Hell, maybe he was.

"Yeah, I see that." I swallowed. "I just don't necessarily know what kind of leader I am when I'm not tryin' to be like her."

Javier let go of my foot, ignoring my noise of displeasure at the abandoned massage, and pulled me over to straddle his lap. "You don't need to know right now, Hannah. You've got a long time to lead. A long, long time."

"Yeah, you're right." I rested my head on his shoulder. "I don't plan on dyin' anytime soon, not before I get all those babies you promised me, at least."

He kissed my breath away, his lips and tongue making me feel happy and comforted in the exact way I needed just then.

"Maybe I can ask your daddy for help," I said when we pulled apart. "It's fine to ask your father-in-law for help, right? Even if he is your rival?"

I had my hands on his face, framing his bearded cheeks as we stared at each other. He was so singularly handsome, I never wanted to take my eyes or hands off him. The fact that he was a good man—a man who supported me and loved me and set me on fire—overwhelmed me even more.

"I don't think we can call ourselves rivals anymore, wife." Javier laughed. "Not after today. We were bonded together on that mountain. Everything changes after this."

"I guess that means y'all don't have to rush to get out of our hair then," I told him. "Everybody'll be too busy talkin' about what a badass I was today to fight until you guys get your kitchen back up and runnin'."

"Oh, I think they'll always find a reason to fight." He laughed. "Just...now, they'll do it as siblings instead of enemies."

"Shit, I'll take it, just as long as you keep breakin' them up instead of me."

"Always," he breathed.

I cuddled into him even more, finding comfort in his warmth. "We need to go visit Sam in the hospital tomorrow," I said after a long stretch of silence. "Cam sent me a picture of him in his hospital bed with this big goofy smile on his face. He's fine, but I want to see him in person to make sure."

"Look at you, carin' about my people," Javier said with a smirk.

"Sam is a sweet kid, and he took a bullet for the cause. Actually, maybe we need to get him a gift too."

"Think we could get him a white Porsche like the one the Wards have?"

I snorted. "Maybe one of those tiny Hot Wheels models."

"Knowing him, he'd still be grateful for it."

"Maybe a promotion would be better. One for him and

Cam both. It would show the rest of our people that unity gets rewarded."

Javier looked down at me with a small smile on his lips. His eyes darkened. "I don't think I'll ever get tired of watchin' you be a boss."

"Shut up." I shoved my body back against him. "You probably just want me to boss you around a little bit."

"Maybe so."

"Probably more than a little bit."

The second my lips met his, my fatigue went away and all I could think about was my husband—handsome and supportive...and *mine.*

# EPILOGUE

JAVIER

*Six Months Later*

A lot of people didn't understand the purpose of a homegoing celebration instead of a funeral. On the surface, they were incredibly similar—a packed church full of crying people dressed in all black, ominous organ music, and even the quintessential mourning foods. The big difference came after all that. After family and friends left the church behind for a spot much more appropriate for drinking and cursing and carrying on.

In true Kentucky style, that spot for us was a barn. The same place Hannah and I had celebrated our binding was the same place we celebrated Miss Clara's life.

I hadn't known the woman well. In the months after the showdown with the Wards and before her death, I'd met her only three times. But I got the distinct feeling this was exactly what she would have wanted.

Her funeral had taken place at her home church in Louisville as had her main repast. But the Mezas and Hawkins had taken it upon ourselves to honor her in a place where Clyde felt a little more at home.

I couldn't help but take notice that the scene we found ourselves in was more similar to our reception than I'd originally recognized. Our people mingled more, two families joined by food and liquor and dancing in a way much less strained than before. The head table where I sat with Hannah, my parents, and Clyde had much more ease as well, even considering how high emotions were otherwise.

"This new batch is good, son," Clyde commented at me over a half-full glass.

I didn't have it in me to be sheepish as I accepted his compliment. "Thank you. I made this one special for tonight. I remembered Miss Clara mentionin' how much she liked bananas once, so I whipped some up in a base mash to see how it'd turn out."

Hannah, who'd been sipping on a glass of her own, smiled sweetly at me and reached over to run a hand through my hair. "She wasn't much of a drinker, but she would have loved knowin' there was somethin' out there inspired by her."

Clyde kept his eyes on his cup.

"I'll make sure to bottle a batch for you to keep," I said. "For any time you want somethin' special to remember her by."

His thanks came in the form of a harsh nod, but it was enough for me. He was still struggling to get a handle on the torrent of emotions he must have been feeling.

My parents stood up from the table and make their way to the dance floor, holding each other close in that way people did when they got to thinking about death. Clyde turned in his seat, his back to Hannah and I as he looked over the dance floor. She and I weren't alone, but we still had a certain kind of privacy, so I took a moment to drop a kiss on her lips. I was driving, which meant I wasn't drinking, but I could detect the white whiskey on her lips. Whatever deliciousness may have existed in my new batch was only strengthened by the taste of her.

"Is it awful I can't stop thinkin' about how handsome you look in your funeral suit?" she asked once I pulled back.

"Probably." I chuckled. "But you know I'm always ready to hear you compliment me."

"Well, in that case, you look good enough to eat."

"You'll have plenty of time for that later, wife."

Hannah scooted her chair closer to mine and whispered in my ear. "Maybe we can use that time to get to work on those Hawkins-Meza babies too."

I couldn't have masked the shock on my face if I'd tried, nor the enthusiasm. It had been six months since we'd gotten rid of the Wards. To say that things had gone back to normal would have been wrong, largely because they'd been better. I'd put my house up for sale and officially moved into Hannah's place.

The tension that had existed between our families for decades was still there, but it became less heated with each day. The number of fights had dwindled to nearly none, and the number of friendships and bonds had grown exponentially.

Even after the Mezas got our own kitchens back up and running, we continued to work closely with the Hawkins, going on runs together and sharing resources.

The Wards had taught us there was strength in numbers and unity, and we'd taken the lesson and run with it. Our business was still separate in terms of money and operations, but we all knew it wouldn't be that way forever. With Hannah and I sticking together and my parents getting older, it was only a matter of time before we had to join together for real. We didn't have it all figured out yet, but Hannah and I knew having kids would be the start of that.

We'd been joking about it for months, but I'd made it perfectly clear I was ready to start whenever she was. The words she'd whispered in my ear had been flirty, but I knew her well enough by now to know they'd also been serious. I had to stop myself from laying her out on the table right then and there.

"I'm not so sure I agree with that hyphenation." I swallowed. "I think 'Meza' needs to go first."

The look on Hannah's carried a bit more weight once she heard my words.

She stood up out of her chair, put her glass on the table, and straightened out the long black dress she wore. "I don't want to wait until we get home." She held a hand out to me. "Let's go to the truck now."

"Right now?" I looked at our surroundings, at Clyde. "At a funeral?"

"What better way to celebrate death than by making a new life?"

Her words were wild and maybe even a little offensive, but they still made me hot. I stood up too, taking one of her soft hands in mine before leading us towards the entrance of the barn.

"Have I told you how much I love you lately, wife?"

She was slightly behind me, so I couldn't see her face, but I could hear the dirty grin in her voice. "Yeah, but now I want you to show me."

CPSIA information can be obtained
at www.ICGtesting.com
Printed in the USA
FSHW011021260420
69614FS

9 781733 426565

7